Convenient Beauty

Asata Benjamin

Also by Asata Benjamin

Beauty Regency Series
Hidden Beauty
Blind Beauty

Convenient Beauty

A Novel
A Beauty Regency Novella, Book Three

Asata Benjamin
Kademete Books

Convenient Beauty

A Beauty Regency Novella, Book Three

Copyright © 2022 by Asata Benjamin

Cover design by Broken Candle Book Designs

Editing and Formatting by Tamara Eaton

Visit our website at www.Kademete.com

ISBN: 978-1-7359256-2-2

Dedication

In loving memory of Terry Burrow.

Prologue

1834, On the Battlefield

THE CRIES OF ANGUISH were drowned out by the muskets penetrating their target. The sounds swept through the air filled with the smell of burning bodies, the iron balls filled with gunpowder and the torches, their enemies burnt. Smoke fogged the atmosphere, bringing a dark, eerie glow to the approaching dawn. Lord Cayden Knights, Fifth Earl of Caswell, England lay beneath the heavy burden of lifeless bodies, his solemn gaze cast upon the cloudless sky, yearning for death to swept him away from his aching, weak body.

He was unaware if it was his blood he felt trickling down his abdomen or the person on top of him--not just any person. A lonely tear, formed at the corner of his eye, disappearing at the sudden movement of his eyes closing--his best friend, Eric Angus, third son of the Duke of Willowdon. They had been inseparable since infancy, Eric always tagging along wherever Cayden went. Eric took punishments for him, as Cayden had always been considered weak as a child. At times he wondered if Eric's shadowing had been as a way of protection. Nevertheless, he always welcomed the blue eyes that resembled a calm sea. Cayden eyes opened, saturated with tears like a dry well on a rainy day as he recalled the unfortunate outcome. If only he had seen that wounded soldier about to shoot that iron ball--if only he hadn't stopped in the middle of battlements to reload his musket. If only Eric had let him die instead.

"Cayden!"

He blinked back tears, lips unwilling to move, to cry to alert his brother of his whereabouts. "Cayden, where the devil are you?"

Upon hearing the shuffling of footsteps drawing nearer, Cayden slid his eyes closed. The world around him disappeared. If only for a moment, he could pretend that it was just a nightmare. He felt a looming shadow hovering over him. Was it one of the enemy?

"Oh, dear brother, it was always meant to be like this."

Cayden was too stunned to move as his brother reached over and snatched the silver chain off his neck. A chain bearing their family crest. A chain his father had given him on his death bed. A chain he should be buried with upon his death.

Why was his brother taking it? Perhaps it was to take back to his mother as proof of his death?

Cayden waited until his brother left and his eyes flew open. There was no sadness in his brother's voice. No sobbing of mourning his young brother's death. His pondering on his brother's affection towards him halted when one of his fellow soldiers dropped beside him. He pivoted his head to see the soldier clutching his side as blood oozed from between his fingers.

"I hate the bloody war!" the soldier cursed, before his brown eyes met dark blue ones. "Cayden?" Bloody hands reached out and grabbed at his lapels.

Cayden winced when he was pulled from his cushion of confinements. The pain was excruciating and his leg; he couldn't feel anything in his left leg!

"You are one serendipitous sonafabitch!" His saviour paused to shoot at the enemy before turning back to him, a triumphant smile on his face. "It's time to get you to safety, my friend."

Cayden didn't want to be saved...He wanted to die.

Chapter One

1835, Lady Wyne's Ballroom, England.

PRINCESS ROSEMARY RICHMOND of Blackmane, was not one to be driven to the point of frustration. However, after spending hours trying to find the right words to finish the last three chapters in her novel, she was ready to scream. She had sacrificed a year writing her book, a scandalous book that went against everything society deemed as proper. *Romance.* The noises in the ballroom did little to calm her nerves as the blabbing became vividly loud; laughter, clashing of champagne glasses and the prancing of boots and slippers on the marble flooring.

A stubborn dark curl fell over her forehead. A fine job her lady's maid had done of securing it, although it might have been her fault for being so antsy during the preparations. The curl blocked the words she had been staring at for the past few minutes. Idly, Rosemary swatted it away, only for it to irritate her even more when it fell back into her line of view.

"Stop it!" she whispered, as if scolding a naughty child. "I'm trying to concentrate!" She sounded like a madwoman, talking to a strand of hair. A chuckle escaped her lips, and she quickly covered a hand over her mouth when someone beside the table asked the other if they heard that distinct noise.

Rosemary's eyes widened. She could not be found laughing to herself under the refreshment table. *Perhaps if they thought her mad, she wouldn't be dragged to another Ball by her grandmother?* Rosemary mentally shook that thought away. The curl, as if reading her mind, acted without consent and fell over her forehead. She groaned wearily. The possibility of her never attending another Ball without tarnishing her family's reputation was very slight. She was already travelling down a scandalous road with her writings. It was frowned upon by everyone, especially her grandmother, who had done everything in her power to keep Rosemary occupied during her first season in London. Grandmother had tried to distract her from scribbling in her journal. It was only natural that Rosemary found a place to hide to keep up with her leisure activity.

"I think it came from under the table?" A feminine voice said to her partner.

Rosemary didn't know anyone at this Ball. It was just one of those events her grandmother brought her to find suitors and try to get her to make acquaintances. London was new to her; she had spent all her years at Blackmane Castle with her cousins and family. The people of London, despite previous assumptions, were very friendly, and everyone appeared to want her as their companion. Rosemary knew it was because she was Royal, and she detested false modesty. How could she ever find true friendship among a bunch of pretentious persons in the bustle of the city? She loved the countryside and the quietness of it all. However, she enjoyed her freedom away from the castle, where everyone treated her like a fragile glass. Here, with her grandmother, she could be herself, walk long distances without numerous guards, climb trees and most importantly write.

All with the sacrifice of attending every Ball.

Rosemary crawled out from the back of the table, standing just in time to witness the lady raising the cloth slightly, to peek under it. She bit back laughter when the lady's male companion looked heavenward, realizing how silly it was to even think that someone would have been hiding under there.

Folding the leather coverlet of her journal, Rosemary tucked the feather quill inside and went searching for another hiding place. When she saw Lady Richmond, her grandmother, advancing with two older companions at her side, one was the hostess of the Ball, Lady Wyne. Rosemary ducked behind a white pillar.

The matchmaking matchmakers, she giggled at her witty thought.

"You must assist me at once to find her, ladies, before what's left of the eligible bachelors disappear from this bore of a party." Her grandmother's voice caught a few onlookers, but she gave them no attention. "I am thinking very seriously about using my old tricks especially the one I used on my dear son."

Rosemary's eyebrows crunched. When would her grandmother's quest to find her a husband end? She didn't want a husband; she just wanted to finish her book and write more. Marriage wasn't on her mind. She had already turned down all the gentlemen who had asked for a dance. As she took a step from the pillar and looked around the ballroom, she noted it was slowly emptying of not just gentlemen, but everyone. A smile lingered on her lips. The Ball would finish soon, and she'd be on her way home, dreaming of the comforts of her bedchamber where she could put quill to paper without disturbance. Lost in her thoughts, she was interrupted by her grandmother's voice.

"Rose!"

Rosemary winced. She turned just in time to see her grandmother stomping towards her, her white silk gown trying desperately to keep up with her pace, as she was very energetic for a lady of her age. A grin spread across Rosemary's face and before Lady Richmond could forbid her not to do it, Rosemary took off running. She ignored the loud shout of warnings and the bewildered onlookers that stepped out of her way. She raced out of the ballroom, onto a balcony, and down the stairs into a garden. Rosemary had always enjoyed playing hide and seek with her grandmother although her behaviour might be childish. It was positively devious and...exciting.

Chapter Two

ORD CAYDEN KNIGHTS IGNORED the slight pain in his leg as he made himself comfortable on the wooden bench in the garden. He wiggled his upper body, trying to find a comfortable spot. Who made this bench so uncomfortable by the way? He grumbled, sighing when he found some sort of comfort.The cretinous Ball would soon be over anyway, he'd just have to endure until it ended. Since he came back from the war, his mother's endless nagging to get him married kept him wishing he was dead. Home was not peaceful anymore and to make matters worse, he had to leave the house to put up with this pretentious charade of attending Balls to make his mother happy. At every event, he dressed, showed up, and immediately familiarized himself with the hostesses' gardens and spent the night in the solitude of the darkness, where he wallowed in sorrow and despair.

Not again...because after tonight. He wouldn't be around.

There was an odd noise in the distance, the crunching of leaves and feminine giggling. It was not the first time a couple came out in the garden for a late-night tryst. He disregarded the noise, too slothful to move. Not caring if they saw him, he'd stay where he was. If they did, they would leave, and he might be able to reward himself for stopping a liaison that might have ended badly. The intentions of gentlemen that brought ladies out in the wilderness for short thrills were never good. *But wasn't he one of those gentlemen before?* The footsteps grew louder until they were upon him.

"Oh sir, I didn't see you there!"

He refused to acknowledge the startled voice.... *ignore it and it will go away.*

He was so wrong.

"Sir? Are you alright?" The footsteps grew nearer until the lady was standing over him and it didn't end there. The dratted woman started to poke him with a stick!

"Leave me woman!" he growled, lifting his hand, and swatting the stick away, also refusing to open his eyes. He did hear the stick contacting the ground but no footsteps running away.

"Oh, great. You aren't dead. I was just about to bury you in the garden. Surely no one would miss such a lonely vile man," she drawled softly. "Or perhaps that would be too cruel—for the plants in garden, of course. You know, if the soil is bad, plants cannot grow properly."

Lord help him, he was going to take a life before ending his.

"Oh, you look mighty uncomfortable on that bench. It's too small for you, sir. Why don't you just lie on the ground?"

His eyes flew open, and his intention to protest angrily at her intrusion got stuck in his throat as he stared into green jewels of quite possibly the most beautiful woman he had ever laid eyes upon.

She stared back at him, equal astonishment on her face.

"Rose!" a voice called.

Dark curls that hung loosely around her face swayed as she turned to the entrance. He frowned at the distant voice.

Another intrusion? Can't a man wallow with guilt in peace?

"Oh dear!" She swung back, looking eagerly around the tiny, secluded area. "I have to hide under this bench, please don't tell anyone you saw me!" Before he could comprehend or find his voice, the lady was crawling under the bench just as another came into view. This one was much older, but equally beautiful. Cayden sat upright immediately and hissed at the pain in his leg.

There would be no more after tonight, he reprised.

No more pain.

No more sorrow.

Just peace.

"Good evening, my lord." The old lady curtseyed, eyes not wavering from his. "You won't by chance have seen a young lady come this way?"

"No, I'm afraid not." He coughed as if to hide his guilt. Why was he lying for this strange lady? "Is she lost?" The concern in his voice and curious expression would have made him a popular actor if he ever had joined the theatre.

The older lady shook her head. "No," She waved her hand dismissively. "She's a mischievous little minx, and I'm getting too old chasing her," she mumbled, then smiled at him. "I don't remember seeing you in the ballroom. And is this where all the handsome bachelors resign to escape nagging mothers and such?" The lady's eyes slowly moved around the darkness apprehensively as if expecting to see more gentlemen or something else emerge from the garden.

"I-" He sputtered, lost for words.

"Oh, it doesn't matter, you must be introduced to my granddaughter." The old lady clapped her hands together with glee, her teeth glittering in the moonlight. "Just as soon as I find her." She turned to leave then swung back around, with an index finger in the air. "What's your name, my lord?"

Cayden who was already wearing a scowl on his face, replied with as much politeness as necessary. He hated a matchmaker. "Lord Cayden Knights, Earl of Caswell."

ROSEMARY HELD HER BREATH as she listened to the stranger converse with her grandmother. She didn't release it until they were left alone.

"Oh, thank you, sir," she exclaimed, crawling from under the bench, she jumped to her feet, pushing her long fallen curls behind her ears.

She looked at the stranger, blond hair brushed his shoulders, smooth and silky as it shone under the moonlight. His dark blue eyes were shadowed by long thick lashes. It didn't stop her from noticing how cold they were or how handsome he was. She wouldn't even dare mention his pink plump lips, stubborn pointed nose. Oh dammit, she couldn't look away!

The silence continued until the handsome Earl cleared his throat, snapping her out of her dreamy trance. "I suggest you leave now before someone else comes and finds you with a stranger," he said dismissively, leaning back on the bench and closing his eyes.

Rosemary would not be dismissed like a servant; she folded her arms and glared at him.

"Why are you still here?" He peeked through one eye.

"I wish to thank you for not telling my grandmother where I was."

"Your apology for disturbing my peace is accepted," he said dryly.

Rosemary's frown deepened as he closed his eyes on a sigh.

"Stop fishing for apologies," she exclaimed.

"Stop annoying me," he retorted with annoyance.

"Are you always this insulting to ladies? I am only trying to be nice, not apologize, for I did nothing to offend you."

"Only the ladies that don't know when they are dismissed. Your entire presence is offending."

She plucked a rose flower and tossed it at him.

His eyes flew open as the flower smacked him in the face. He sat upright, sluggishly and seeming to take extra care in righting his left leg. "I was trying to be discreet in my dismissal, but I see that isn't working, so would you please leave me alone for heaven's sake!" he bellowed.

She wished she had thrown the roses with thorns on them instead.

"The Ball is a terrible bore, and I am in need of some fresh air," she said, ignoring his outburst. She didn't want to return to her grandmother quite yet and somehow, she was drawn to this mysterious stranger. Rosemary got the impression that he was a very lonely man, likely because of his lack of social skills.

"The stars are lovely tonight—"

"Oh, heavens take me now," he muttered.

"---I have never seen so many before," she continued, as she looked to the skies with a sigh. It was a lie of course--she had indeed seen a lot more stars than what were out tonight, but conversation was necessary. She heard him swear repeatedly and turned to him. "Why are you so angry sir? The garden is big enough for two."

"And yet you are still here."

"Caswell."

He lifted an eyebrow in a look of sheer bewilderment, for using his name.

"Lord Caswell," she continued.

"And what's the significance of you repeating my name?"

"It's to remind you whose garden you are in, Lady Wyne's. You trying to persuade me to leave doesn't account for anything." She shrugged.

"I am this close to strangling you," he mumbled, eyes burning with irritation. "Please return to the Ball and occupy yourself with snatching a husband or whatever you ladies do for entertainment."

CAYDEN ROLLED HIS EYES when the lady, Rose, he assumed, let out a long sigh.

"That's the problem, I don't want to go back." She hung her head, looking everywhere but at him and that's when he noticed she was hiding tears.

Something tugged at his heart seeing her like this, but he said nothing. Where were these feelings coming from? She was a mere stranger. Why should he care about her?

"Everyone wants me to marry but I don't. I just want to be left alone to write." On another sigh she strolled towards him and took a seat on the bench.

Her distance was too close, and he rose to his feet.

She looked up at him a tiny smile spreading across her mouth. "Can I not stay here with you? You looked like you need some company."

Yes, she was insane. If he wanted company he would be in the blasted ballroom! Cayden looked at the lady incredulously. "What gave you that impression?" he drawled sarcastically. "I'm a man and you are a lady, and we are alone in a dark secluded garden." He gripped the back of the bench beside her shoulders, and he leaned towards her. When she lifted her head to stare at him, his face was mere inches from hers. "I can easily take advantage of you right here."

She swallowed. "You wouldn't." Her gaze drifted to his lips.

"How can you be so sure?" he whispered.

"Because, if you did, you'd have to marry me, and you look like the sort that doesn't want to be compromised. Why else would you be hiding out here in the garden?" Rosemary smiled, and he stood upright.

He loathed the fact that she was right and read him so easily.

"Why does marriage scare you?" he asked. "Every lady wants to marry; spinsterhood is shunned upon and such a great burden to bear."

"I never said it did." She rose, took a step past him, then turned around. "I just need time, to finish my books."

"Now see here, you are giving up a family, children, the marital bed for books?" His eyebrows rose.

"Well, you can't possibly expect a lady to write with all those distractions, do you?" She placed her hands on her hips and glared at him. "What about you, sir? Why do you detest marriage?"

Cayden thought for a moment. With going off to the army, he never really thought about marriage. He didn't want the burden of a lady waiting back home to distract him on the battlefield. Now he was home, wishing he was dead, while his mother was on his back to get married. The thought only brought melancholy. How could he live and enjoy life when his best friend was dead because of him?

Finally he said, "Marriage to me would be a burden, and I can't tell my mother otherwise for she would be devastated, and the nagging would grow more intense."

That's why he had to leave.

Rosemary nodded understandingly as she twirled her curls between her fingers. She watched him retreat to the bench.

She was silent for a moment before her eyes suddenly widened. "Oh my gosh, I have an idea!" She rushed to sit beside him. "Let's get married!"

Cayden was suddenly glad that he wasn't standing. He stared at the lady like she had two heads. Did she just say those words? Propose to him? A total stranger? "You, my lady, are insane. I'm leaving."

She surged to her feet, preventing him from rising by standing in front of him.

"No, no, please allow me to speak," she said hastily.

"Haven't you been doing that for the past few minutes?" he asked.

She narrowed her eyes. The more she stayed in his company the more he was reading into her character. "I know this may seem too soon, but it's the solution to *our* problem. Your mother's nagging would disappear, and I'll get to write without my grandmother dragging me to these events." Her eyes rolled at that remark, and she began pacing while she continued to explain herself. "It would be a marriage of convenience. We wouldn't actually be a true married couple. You can still go about your reckless pitiful ways, and I'll finally have peace to write." She turned to him with glee, hope shimmering in her eyes. "What are your thoughts of a marriage of convenience?"

Cayden kept staring at the lady, his voice lost in his throat. A marriage of convenience? No more motherly nagging? A sham wife and a beautiful one at that? Beautiful and utterly mad, and if she kept looking at him like that he just might agree to be as mad as her. Which part of he didn't wish to be married did she not understand? Had he stammered or something?

"I believe I have made myself clear. No marriage is in the future for me, convenience or not. I cannot marry you," He growled, then stomped away, or in his situation, limped. He could not listen to any more of this nonsense.

She ran in front of him, preventing him from moving. "My Lord, please think it through--"

"Ummm.....let me see." He placed one hand on his hips and pretended to be deep in thought. "Oh, I have made a decision! And the answer is still no!" Rose glared at him, he moved to the left and she moved with him, he attempted to try the right and she followed.

"I will not let you leave!" Her foot hit the ground with so much force, she winced.

"Ha, as if you can stop me!"

"We could put that to the test, if I had a rope and a knife." She stuck her chin in the air. "Do you mind staying here until I return with the items?"

"You know what you need? A doctor not a husband, poor gentleman would slit his throat before he could make it to church," he said, glaring down at her.

"Well at least he'd have the courage to agree to attempt to make it to the church."

He'd had enough of this!

A scream left her mouth when she was lifted and tossed over his shoulder, effortlessly. "Put me down, you beast!" Her fist beating his back did little to hinder his progress of leaving the garden and climbing the stairs. "I might inform you that you are risking your life as we speak! I'll have you hang for this!"

"First you speak of marriage, then murdering me?" He smirked. "Are you sure we aren't married already? I wouldn't put it past you to drug me to get leg-shackled."

"Oh, now that's an idea!" she exclaimed.

"Rose!"

Cayden suddenly placed her on the pavement as her grandmother appeared on the balcony.

"You naughty young lady! Where have you been!" She turned to Cayden her eyes narrowing.

He lifted his hands in the air in mock surrender. "I remembered you were searching for your granddaughter. I merely acted accordingly," he said. "A young lady such as her shouldn't be walking the gardens talking and giggling to herself."

Rosemary gasped. "You--" She tried to launch at him, but her grandmother gripped her arm, pulling her back.

"How many times must I tell you not to speak to yourself?" the grandmother said in a hushed tone.

"And giggle," he interrupted, looking sympathetically at her.

Rose's jaw clenched.

"You should really find her a husband before it's too late and word gets out."

"'You, vile pathetic bore!" she spat.

Cayden made his departure then, leaving the grandmother to discipline her granddaughter. He smiled all the way to his carriage and instructed his coachman to hasten his journey back to the Caswell Estate. It was time to do what must be done, what he had planned for months since his return to England. But why was he feeling doubtful suddenly?

Chapter Three

ROM THE SOFT CUSHION-PADDED seat of the carriage, Cayden lifted the red drapes and found peace in the breathtakingly view of the Caswell manor. The decorated lanterns that stuck out from the wall like grasses sprouting from the ground always made him feel peaceful, assurance that there would always be light in darkness. The orange hue brightened its surroundings like a magnificent sunset, bringing attention to the manor. It was times like these he cherished the most, when he could admire the lush beauty of his ancestral home. His father would have hated it, he thought with a lingering smile, thinking of the play on words his father would have used to talk them out of such wastage. Truthfully, it took a lot of oil and workmanship to light each one every night and each morning expel those that had lasted through the darkness. But it was worth it.

The smile slipped from his face. What would his father say, if he knew of his son's weakness? What was about to transpire tonight? He had always been physically weak as a child, and his parents had loved him unconditionally. This, however, was different—he no longer was striving for survival. The will was gone; his mind was the weak one now, not his body. The horses came to a halt, drawing him out of his reverie. With a sigh, he released the drapes, his gaze drifting to the carriage's door.

Servants came to the door, greeting him with a smile as he stepped out. One took his coat, the other took the hat that rested under his arm. This ludicrous act was his father's rule, one that they kept merely out of respect, stripping him before he reached inside. *'Taking the burdens and evening events off his shoulders before entering the house,'* his father would say. It never worked with him and, as he stepped foot in the foyer, a sense of dread washed over him. He was giving all this up, never to see it again. With trembling fingers, he glided them against the railing and took slow steps up the stairs.

How he wished to see his mother standing at the top waiting for him, but the soundless echo of the house told him she had already retired. As the servants busied themselves downstairs before retiring as well, Cayden stood at the entrance of his bedchamber for a second, but it felt like an eternity. The creak of a door pushing open reached him, then footsteps travelled towards him.

"Aros, I thought I told you not to wait up for me!" He gritted the words through his teeth, kicking the door shut with a boot.

His valet paused, noticing his livid expression. "My lord, forgive me but it's in my interest that I see you out of those boots before I could rest peacefully."

Cayden pinched the bridge of his nose. "If it pleases you," he murmured, taking a seat on the edge of the bed. "My apologies for raising my voice."

Aros gave him a small smile before scrunching on his knees and taking one booted leg in his hands. "It's rare to see you angry, my lord. The Ball was not to your liking?"

Cayden groaned, dropping his upper body back on the mattress. "It wasn't all bad." He smiled, remembering the beautiful blunt young lady. "I met a lady." He was vaguely aware of the slight pause in the young valet's tugs at his boot. "A quite peculiar young lady, one that had bats in the head too, if you must ask me."

Aros chuckled. "She must have left quite an impression. It's rare for you to return from a Ball and speak of a lady. It must have gone well."

Cayden didn't address the correctness of that statement. Aros knew everything about him, except his thoughts about life. Pretending to attend Balls, but taking residence in a brothel or pub instead was something that did cross his mind. But his mother always found a way to know if he attended. Her advantage was knowing all the hostesses.

With a sigh from Aros, one that sound more like contentment than frustration, he gave a final tug, and boot was removed. He moved to the other. "My lord?"

Cayden sat upright immediately. "What is it?"

"I'm about to take off the other boot."

Cayden swallowed then slightly nodded. His hands dug into the white sheet at the pain travelling up his leg. His teeth gritted, as he watched Aros pull and tug and twist.

"Christ, hurry with it man!"

Aros fell back two paces with the boot in hand. "Got it!" His valet, said out of breath.

Cayden sighed, wiggling his toes. "Thank you." He would never have gotten that off by himself.

"You're welcome, my lord." Gathering the boots off the ground, Aros moved to tuck them away from sight. "My Lord, do you wish to speak more of this young lady?" He slammed the wardrobe door closed, made his way to the wash basin, and filled a bowl with water.

Cayden thought for a second, pulling his shirt over his head and tossing it on the floor. Did he want to converse with his valet about the lady? Pivoting his head, he watched as Aros came towards him, his nightly ritual of cold water to wash his hands and face before bed.

"Aros, what would I ever to do without you?"

"I do not wish to find out, my lord."

He smiled, accepting the water. "As to the young lady, she was quite insolent, called me a pathetic boor."

Aros mouth hung open. "A lady called you a boor, that's absurd!"

Cayden sinking his face in the water. He chuckled, as his face resurfaced. "She's no ordinary lady, Aros." He accepted the cloth thrust at him, slapping it at his face until he was dry. "Quite blunt, not a trait from a respectable lady. I suppose her family is only in the aristocratic circle because of pity, for no lady of high stature would have spoken so rudely." He snorted, swinging his legs on the bed. "I believe that will be all, Aros."

His valet hesitated, staring at him as if he wanted to ask more and with a nod, he bid his master goodnight. Cayden hoisted himself on his elbow and reached into the wooden drawer, taking the tiny bottle out. He squeezed it in his palm and rested his head back on the soft pillow.

How simple this task tonight was to be—drink and never wake up again. Yet something was holding him back. Was it the look on his mother's face when she realized what he had done? Every time he closed his eyes, he saw the expression. Horror. It would crush her heart. Or was it the thought that his brother would be Earl?

It was Hugh's birth right, and no one would question that, except perhaps the Will his father had drafted before his death. Why he placed Cayden as his heir instead was strange. Truthfully, his brother could be very temperamental and drink excessively at times, but he was always kind to him.

Except that one incident... The recollection sent a chill through his body, and he still felt the heavy weight on his chest, Eric's body. With a sigh, he closed his eyes and reached for the pendant, only to realize his brother hadn't ever given it back. Hugh didn't even mention that he had it, and Cayden wasn't going to reveal that he knew Hugh did. It was simple. Hugh felt cheated out of the heirloom and always wanted it. Why not let him have it? It was just a pendant anyway--A pendant, his father had given him when he was of age. A pendant he had always touched for comfort and reassurance.

Then there was Rose, the lady he met such a short time ago. He didn't know why, but she intrigued him. Recalling the abrupt marriageable proposal, Cayden chuckled. He never thought he would live to see the day, and he wondered how far she was willing to go with this charade. Opening his palm, he held the bottle in the air between his thumb and index finger. He stared at it for a while, until the candlelight dimmed. Then, with a groan of defeat, he reopened the drawer, threw the bottle inside, and slammed it shut, leaving an echoing, empty feeling in the room.

Putting it off one more night wouldn't hurt.

THE NEXT MORNING CAYDEN met his mother sitting alone in the parlour with freshly brewed chamomile tea, toast, and butter. Although her favourite snack was displayed, her mind seemed preoccupied, which was why she jumped out of her seat when he called her.

"Cayden!" With trembling hands, she touched her chest. "You...you scared me!"

"My apologies." He kissed her cheek tenderly. "May I join you for some toast, Mother?"

Lady Caswell slowly took a seat and managed to return the small smile he bestowed upon her. "If I ask, Lesley will find something more to satisfy your appetite." As she said this, he was already buttering a slice.

"It's no trouble, Mother," His words were muffled by a huge bite of toast. "I'm actually going out in a while."

This caused Lady Caswell's eyebrows to shoot upwards. His mouth to twitch into a smirk. He always remained in his chamber after a Ball, never to be seen unless his mother forced herself into his room. Cayden was also never this cheerful and outgoing, so his mother's astonishment was understandable.

"May I inquire as to your destination, son?" One curious blonde brow lifted.

"Yes, Mother, you may." He poured himself some tea. "In fact, you might want to put the tea down."

Lady Caswell's mouth hovered over the china teacup before, with a grim expression, she did what he said. "Surprises can be both lovable and disastrous. You know how I detest them, Cayden." Though, it was the truth, he heard the eagerness in her voice.

"Well...perhaps you are right. You need not hear about this then," he said nonchalantly, concentrating on his light breakfast. He tried to ignore the gaze of his mother, but he couldn't resist looking then bestowed on her a mischievous smile.

The corners of her mouth twitched before transforming into a broad smile. "Cayden Knights! Stop teasing your mother and tell me what it is!"

Unfortunately, she would have to wait a while longer as Hugh burst into the room.

"Oh brother, you are here." Cayden smiled at Hugh's startled expression. Everyone was acting like he shouldn't be here. If they did find his poison, he wasn't alarmed for he had spoken about death more often in the past couple of months. They knew he didn't want to be alive. They knew the heartache he was in after Eric's death. Of course, his mother had thought he just needed to get married and such feelings would disappear.

It would never...but perhaps he should try.

Hugh was dishevelled—spending his nights at the tavern while drinking away their father's money was a routine. His jacket and waistcoat were missing to complement his white linen shirt. As Hugh dragged a chair to sit between them, Cayden could see one of the buttons from his breeches was missing. "It's a lovely day, isn't it?" He grinned, leaning back on the chair. "Mother, you look beautiful today. As always, blue really brings out your eyes."

"Stop it!" His mother's sweet voice rose an octave as she glared at his brother. Cayden didn't like seeing her upset. The lines on her forehead always wrinkled and her eyes looked like she would erupt with tears any minute. "If you continue with this behaviour, I'll have no choice but to cut you off for good! I am tired of you coming home like this!" In disgust she waved her hands towards Hugh. "Ever since you came back from the war, it has gotten worse!" Lady Caswell surged to her feet, chest heaving.

"At least I'm not trying to kill myself like Cayden!" Hugh bellowed. "Would you have mourned more for him than me, if we both didn't return, Mother?" he sneered.

His mother gasped and fell back in the chair. "How dare you!"

"Hugh!" Cayden growled. This rift between Hugh and their mother about whom she treasured more was getting out of control. It had become continuous for Hugh since his return. His mother loved them both, though it was true that she and Cayden shared a bond that Hugh didn't. But that was only because of Hugh's character and the path he took in life, always shying away from holding a conversation or spending time with Mother. Hugh was always behind their father, grooming to be the next Earl. How unfortunate for him that it was all for naught. Cayden wanted to give his title to Hugh, but everyone said it was impossible; even the King, which he had always found strange.

His brother turned to him. "This is all your fault, if only you had gotten married or something, Mother wouldn't be so upset!" The feet of the chair scraped against the floor as he stood.

"That's so like you, Hugh, blaming others for your recklessness! And you don't have to worry about me finding a wife, because I already have!" Cayden realized what he just said when the room suddenly grew quiet. Two pairs of blue eyes were staring wide at him. *Heavens!* This was not how it was supposed to happen and not yet anyway.

"Wife, you say?" Hugh was gaping at him now.

Cayden couldn't believe it himself. *But, in for a penny, in for a pound.*

Straightening his waistcoat, Cayden cleared his throat discreetly. "Yes. In fact, I'm on my way to Hyde Park, to meet her." That wasn't necessarily true. He didn't even know her family name or where she lived. Was Rose even her real name? He was merely going to linger at the park, hoping the lady showed or do some investigations of his own. "Mother, I think you should breathe."

Lady Caswell exhaled a long breath. "Cay-Cayden?"

Cayden went to kiss her on the forehead. "It's the truth, Mother. I have found myself a bride." Tears welled in his mother's eyes. "I'll explain everything on my return," he whispered to her with a smile.

With the same smile on his face, he turned towards his brother. "I'd best be on my way. Can't keep the lady waiting." Whistling to himself, he slipped out of the parlour, leaving them gaping at him. Hugh's sudden laughter that he had lost his mind followed him.

The smile slipped off Cayden's face as he took his hat from the butler. *Perhaps he already has.*

Chapter Four

OSEMARY WAS IN A very irritated mood this morning, as she took deep steady breaths and strolled around Hyde Park. Her grandmother's punishment was much to blame. Taking away her writing materials, leaving her to only dwell on her thoughts, and not have the privilege to scribble them down was ludicrous! How was she to survive an entire week like this? She took a seat on the vacant bench. The park was not as busy as she had thought. After a Ball, it usually was full of activity, which was why she was allowed to get some fresh air. Crowds were limited to Balls, soirees, and theatre. At other events she must walk with guards. Fortunately today, was an exception because of the scarcity of people. Following a night filled with dancing and chatting, most were at home.

No entertainment was here to amuse her; she knew that, but her desire to get away from her grandmother was too strong. She turned and smiled at her carriage where the footmen and chaperone, stood, looking anxiously at the approaching carriage. Without guards from the palace on duty, they took it upon themselves to act as such. Rosemary decided to amuse herself by awaiting the carriage's occupants to make an appearance.

The man that stepped out was impeccably dressed in fine tailor suit. He took off his hat, handing it to the footman, and he ran his hand through his fair hair that ruffled in the wind. By the way his gaze shifted to each of the occupants in the park, he was searching for someone. It was only when he turned in her direction that she recognized who he was.

The boor!

The man who had caused her writing materials to be snatched away. The man who refused her proposal and made her look daft! She stood, hands clinched in fists, when a relieved smile enlightened his face. Slightly limping, he made his way towards her.

"Miss Rose." His voice was smooth as velvet and her eyebrows lifted, with curiosity. "Just the person I wish to see."

"Well, now you have seen me, I must be on my way." She attempted to leave, but he blocked her path, his massive body like a brick.

"Please stay. I wish to discuss our nuptials."

She looked up at him, while discreetly waving at her companions to stay where they were. She wasn't in any danger with this man.

"Sir, did you come here to mock me? Wasn't last night enough to quench your amusement?"

"Last night I was in a horrible mood, couldn't think rationally."

She took a step back, arms folded over her chest. "And now you are?" She eyed him suspiciously.

"Let's sit and discuss this," He motioned to the vacant bench.

"I'd rather stand."

With a shrug, he took the seat. "If you insist."

"I do," she said.

He regarded her with a wry smile. "I came to accept your proposal."

"What?" she screeched, her arms dropping to the side.

"Why is this a shock to you? Did you not propose to me a few hours ago?"

"And I believe you refused," she exclaimed.

"Correction, I didn't refuse—"

"You said no!"

"I just merely thought you were mad," he continued.

She regarded him suspiciously. "But you suddenly now realize I was not?"

His gaze left hers for a moment, as if pondering on that question. "No, you are still quite mad, but I believe we can indeed help each other as you said...We can be mad together." His arms opened wide briefly, as if that explained everything, and he leaned back on the bench.

Rosemary frowned at him for a moment then she took a seat beside him. "You mean get married?" she corrected.

"That's one way of sugarcoating it." He grinned, and her heart leapt at how handsome he was. "Marriage between us is sure to leave one of us mad, we bicker at everything since we have met but, if we stick to the plan you have outlined, our paths won't cross."

She blinked and pretended to stare at her fingers as her mind and heart raced with excitement. Freedom was nearer than she thought. She was going to get married, finally! And the gentleman was gorgeous! Dwelling on his handsomeness was dangerous—for her heart, this marriage, and her thoughts. This was perfect. Her grandmother and parents wouldn't have a say in her writing habits, and she would not be punished for being bashful and blunt. "Fine. Let's get married."

A grin spread across his face. "Excellent!" He got to his feet. "Now tell me your place of residence, and I'll pay a visit to speak to your father--" He stopped and cleared his throat. "Forgive me but I know nothing of your family."

Rosemary stared at him nervously. "You – don't know, um--I mean--"

"Is Rose your real name?" he asked suspiciously.

"Why yes," she answered hastily. "It's Rosemary."

"Rosemary." He repeated her name like it was a sweet caress. "Beautiful." He gazed down at her, and she inhaled a shaky breath.

"You don't have to pay me any compliments, I already agreed to marry you," she mumbled, pivoting her head so he couldn't see the blush.

"Well, my little harpy." He leaned slightly and lifted her face to look into her eyes. "If you are to be my wife, you have to get use to compliments because there will be a lot of it in this marriage."

Rosemary stared at him. At his touch, her brain forgot how to formulate words, although it was only one finger at her chin, she felt like he was caressing her entire body and to her surprise, he used his thumb to smooth along her bottom lip. She gasped and stood so suddenly that she almost lost her balance.

Cayden reached out and held her around the waist, steadying her. "Are you ill? Do you wish to sit once again?"

Her eyes narrowed, noticing the slight twitch of his mouth. The boor knew what he had done!

She swatted his hands away. "You scoundrel! Are you trying to scare me away with your rakish ways?"

His eyebrows lifted. "Have you forgotten that I came to you? I wanted to see if you'll push me away."

She folded her arms. "That was quite insolent of you. Why did you come, by the way? What changed your mind?"

He shifted from one foot to the next on a sigh. "You were right about us helping each other get rid of our nagging matchmakers. It would make my mother very happy."

"Very well." There was something else he wasn't telling her, but she wouldn't press for it. She had a feeling she wasn't going to get it, anyway. He was still a stranger after all.

"Who are your parents?" he asked, taking a seat back on the bench.

She frowned, realization daunting her. Of course, she had never told him her family name. Since she had not grown up in London, not many people knew who she was. And given the Earl's attitude towards Balls, it was understandable, he didn't know either. She smiled and her heart warmed with the realization that he agreed to marry her without knowing that she was a princess. The light bickering—well, she rather enjoyed having someone speak to her... *normally.*

"I don't think that's important at this moment." She'd continue to enjoy this secrecy for a little bit.

He gaped at her. "You are to become my wife, Rosemary. I deserve to know the family I am marrying into, presuming you already know mine."

She bit her lips; she did know his. Lord Cayden Knights, Fifth Earl of Caswell. A soldier. Unfortunately, that's all she knew.

"I don't care if you are not noble," he said. "You would be my countess upon marriage and with it all its privileges." He glared at her suspiciously. "Are you hiding something?"

"Hiding? I wouldn't say that, just withholding some information in case you are jesting with me,.." she said, lifting her chin.

This caused his frown to deepen. "Miss Rosemary, I give you, my word. In fact, I already told my family about the engagement."

"I must be on my way to inform my parents as well," She did a tiny curtsy. "I'll send you a letter with my address."

"Miss Rosemary!" He stood as she gathered her skirts and took off running towards her carriage.

She stopped and turned to him, out of breath. "Await my invitation, my lord! It will be most surprising!"

Chapter Five

*C*AYDEN WONDERED IF HE had made a mistake visiting his friend, Jude Yale, son of the most honest solicitor in London, but he didn't have anyone else he could trust to share his secrets – to converse with. The incident with his brother on the battlefield still unnerved him and his brother had been even more distant since they returned from the war. Not that they had ever had a perfect relationship to talk about such matters. He was oddly pleased with that. Cayden loved his brother but his behaviour of late was still a bewilderment. It couldn't be because of the title; Cayden had been the Earl since he was ten summers.

He looked wryly at Jude, whose hands were stuck in mid-air, depriving himself from filling the glass to the brim with whiskey. Cayden had just announced that he was getting married. It rendered his friend into utter silence and paralysis.

"I beg your pardon?" Jude sputtered, placing the bottle of whiskey on the desk. He looked over to where Randolph, the seventh Marquess of Rombleton, sat with a frown, for further confirmation that he had indeed heard correctly.

Randolph's eyes were concentrating on Cayden at the moment.

The Marquess was more of a drunk than a rake; his love for the bottle had almost killed him more than once. The pubs refused to serve him spirits of any kind. Cayden suspected that was why he was in Jude's study paying a visit at this time of the day.

The Marquess finally took a huge gulp of his drink and turn his gaze to Jude. "I think I'm going to gag and waste perfectly good whiskey. Knights here said something about marrying some lass."

Jude pushed the bottle of whiskey and glass aside. "I need to be sober for this." He leaned against the desk, arms folded. "Are you jesting?"

Cayden shook his head. "I most certainly I'm not."

"Good heavens, I never thought I'd live to see this!" Excitement overwhelmed Jude's voice and he stood straight. "Ranny, did I not just tell you the other day that I might not live to ever see this day?"

"And yet hear you are alive and kicking," the Marquess drawled.

Cayden bit back laughter.

"When's the wedding? What's her name?" Jude came to sit beside him on the couch, acting like an old hag awaiting gossip. "How did the two of you meet?"

"Her name is probably, 'Help, I'm trapped.'" Jude glared at the Marquess, who was banging his knee at his own joke, before focusing back on him.

"Don't mind him," Jude offered.

"Do I ever?" Cayden said dryly. "And if you must know her name is Rose, and we haven't decided on a date as yet." Not wanting to answer the other question, for he didn't know what sort of story Rose might stir up about their first encounter. Dammit! They should have discussed this.

"Rose, what?" Jude insisted.

"I- I only remembered Rose." Cayden shrugged.

"By, Jove! Did you propose to her drunk?" Jude asked, mouth agape.

"No! She proposed to me!" Cayden didn't intend to say that out loud, at the corner of the study, he heard the splatter of liquid flying in the air followed by fits of coughing. The Marquess was coughing, and it sound serious.

Jude was still gaping at him.

"Aren't you going to—" Cayden pointed a finger at the Marquess.

"Oh, we all know one way or the other liquor will kill him," Jude responded casually. "And this is more important."

Cayden was not sure that it was entirely the liquor's fault.

"She proposed to you and you...accepted?" Jude asked, his eyebrows lifted in the air as he awaited an answer. When none came right away, he continued, "That's highly inappropriate for a female to do such a thing, but at the same time, considering it is you...I suppose we can make an exception. Everyone knows you would have never proposed."

Cayden buried his face in his palms. His reluctance to marry had been voiced many times to his friends. Although this was a marriage of convenience, everyone didn't need to know that. And he hoped to God that Rose kept that part of the agreement between them. It was odd that he had no address or means of contacting her. He'd just have to wait until she sent the blasted letter. He loathed being in these sorts of situations, but since he was doing this only for some amusement before he did away with himself, this was more her charade than his. He guessed he could give her full control over it. But Cayden was no fool. He had seen the lady, and she was too beautiful for her own good. Hopefully, she wouldn't fall in love with him.

He knew he wouldn't, but it would be a challenge to resist her. He had almost kissed her right in the open at Hyde Park.

"Cayden?"

He groaned, lifting his gaze at the authority and sternness in his friend's voice. "Are you doing this to get your mother off your back?"

"That is something I shall welcome, but Jude, this lady is the most gorgeous specimen. She's unlike anyone I have ever met." This was the truth. "She has the deepest shade of green eyes I have ever seen, like green wet grass. Her hair is like midnight that twinkles under the sunlight. Rose is also very blunt, a trait most men would find discouraging, but I adore it." Any more of this pretentious sappy love confession and Cayden might throw up.

Beside him, the Marquess cleared his throat. "Wasted whiskey and sappy confessions. I never thought I'd hate both at the same time." The Marquess snickered. "Next, you'll be quoting Shakespeare, and I'll want to rip my heart out."

"You know what, Randolph? One day you will love a lady more than that bottle, and I pray to God I am still alive to see it." Cayden smirked.

The Marquess snorted. "I'm not like you, Cayden," he muttered, his expression suddenly pained, and Cayden knew he was reliving some distant past, some event that no matter how much he drank he never forgot. The Marquess was much stronger than Cayden. Although he could drink himself to death, he never did. But Cayden wanted to kill himself, to leave this world immediately.

"Rose?"

Cayden turned back to Jude. "Yes, that's her name. Do you know her?" he asked, fishing for any information on his mysterious soon-to-be wife.

Jude shook his head. "I don't suppose I do. Not even with the description you gave."

"I know many Roses!" Cayden's straighten at Randolph's interposing. "My mother has lots of them in her gardens." The Marquess' intoxicating laughter filled the study.

"That's it!" Jude stood, yanked the glass from the Marquess' hand. Some of the contents spilled during the struggle, and he cursed a few times at the mess on his tapestry rug. "It's time for you to go home."

Wobbling, the Marquess stood, Jude grabbing one arm. "Ahh, Cayden, am I invited to the wedding?" he asked before leaving the study.

"If you can be sober for a couple of hours," Cayden replied.

The Marquess' eyes fluttered open and closed. It almost looked like he was thinking, which was rare. "I- I think I can manage," he said before Jude ushered him out of the study.

Cayden gazed out the window as the Marquess' carriage disappeared out of sight.

"Now, Cayden, with the jester gone. I need the truth from you." Jude shut the door behind him and he moved into the room.

Cayden finally turned to him, the man he owed his life. Quite literally. If not for Jude, who saved his life on the battlefield, he wouldn't have been here agreeing to this ludicrous marriage. "It's a marriage of convenience."

"I thought as much." Jude exhaled. After pouring himself a glass of whiskey, he leaned against his desk, with a pensive expression. "This is her idea, which I suppose she had a great explanation to indulge in this marriage. But what I don't know, is why have you agreed?"

"She was desperate, and I was available at the time. I believe if I wasn't the unfortunate gentleman, someone else would have been." He smirked, but his friend didn't waver in his expression.

"Answer my question, Cayden."

Cayden lips pursed. "To make my mother happy."

"Enough with the lies, Cayden!" Jude placed his glass on the table and moved to stand mere inches from him. His jaw stern and eyes blazing with anger, Jude was more upset than Cayden had ever seen. He had always been a merry, calm, and sane person. He also saw through others' poker faces, making him one to fear at the tables.

Cayden looked away and swallowed the lump in his throat. "It's my only chance of entertainment, before I – "

Jude took a step backwards. "After a year of mourning Eric, you still have these thoughts? And you are going to play with this lady's emotions like a game?"

Cayden glared at Jude. "This is already a game to her, Jude! I am not the one that proposed to a stranger! I made myself clear that I didn't wish to get married— "

"Because you never intended to stay around. Tell me, Cayden. She has no idea that you intend to make her a widow when you are done having your fun with her?"

Cayden grasped hold of Jude's waistcoat and pushed him back on the desk. "You know not what you speak!" he said, hovering over his friend. "You think I'm going to touch her and risk having a child I may never see grow? I know what it is like to grow up without a father. I wish that on no one." His eyes grew misty, and he released his friend and took a few steps backwards. "I just wanted to see my mother happy and find amusement in my life before I go. This will also make Rose happy."

"You are selfish, Cayden!" Jude spat, fixing his waistcoat. "You think of only yourself and not how your actions affect others. God sent me to save you that day, and instead of being grateful and doing something good with your life, you want to end it. Perhaps Eric did die in vain because you are nothing but a coward."

He stared at his friend for a long moment. Tears clouded his vision, and then he left without a word. Without the intention of returning.

Chapter Six

ROSEMARY KNELT ON THE garden floor on the Corbourne's Estate, resting her palms on her legs and watched her grandmother cut roses and other flowers and place them in her straw basket. Sometimes she adored taking breaks from her writing to join her grandmother in the garden. She loved the smell of freshly disturbed dirt and how colourful it was. How could she not when her mother had always had her trailing behind her in the gardens at Blackmane Castle? Come to think of it, she had more recollections of time spent in gardens during her childhood than were necessary. An idea suddenly invaded her thoughts; what if she made her female protagonist a botanist? Or perhaps the gentleman? It certainly had nothing to do with gender. Rosemary shook her head. No, she could not possibly change her entire novel because of her love for gardens.

"My dear, what are you thinking of now?"

She smiled fondly. "My childhood and the vast number of times spent in gardens."

"Yes. Your mother was quite obsessive," her grandmother replied with a lingering smile.

"She still is. Grandmother, when will they arrive?" Her family was to arrive at the Estate before the month ended, but they hadn't said what date. She wanted them to be here for the announcement, and it had already been four days since she last saw Cayden. He must have given up waiting for her invitation. Or already found out who she really was.

"Oh, yes I forgot to tell you, dear. They will be here two days from now."

She nodded, content with that answer. "Grandmother." She waited until she had her attention. "Do you think Father will approve of any gentleman of my choice?"

Her grandmother's eyebrows drew together. "Yes. If he's a respectable gentleman, and you love him."

Love? This wasn't a love marriage. And would she welcome the idea of loving this man? He was very handsome and made her weak in the knees at his touch, but he was still a stranger. How could she love a stranger? Besides, this was a marriage of convenience. She proposed it, because it was what she wanted. Only a marriage in name, but why was she having doubts? Craving more? Imagining that she was with her own daughter sitting in the garden, picking flowers while her husband watched from the study?

Good Lord! She wasn't even married yet and already wanted it to be real. Thinking of children? Hadn't she called them distractions from her writing? Another lie, to get what she wanted.

Marriage.

She swallowed the lump in her throat. Should she call off the engagement?

"That reminds me. We have a soiree to attend this afternoon. A friend's son has returned from the Continent," her grandmother continued. "He's very charming and loves to write as much as you, but I'm afraid, the both of you would only concentrate on writing and not the marriage duties—"

"I'm betrothed," Rosemary blurred out.

Her grandmother chuckled. "No, you are not, dear." She picked up the basket and stood. "I would know, as I handle your schedule. You haven't met any gentleman long enough to form an acquaintance."

Rosemary looked to the heavens and stood as well.

"Come along, dear, you should have a nap before—"

"Grandmother, I am getting married," she said sternly, following a few steps behind her.

She inhaled deeply as her grandmother slowly turned, the basket slipping from her hands. "What?"

"His name's Lord Cayden Knights, Earl of Caswell," Rosemary continued. "I am waiting for my parents to arrive to set a date immediately." As the words left her mouth, her grandmother's eyes travelled to her midsection.

"Oh my God, you have been ruined right under my nose!"

Rosemary's eyes grew large. "No, Grandmother!"

Lady Corbourne grabbed hold of her arm and began dragging her back to the manor. "How could you let this happen? Oh, people will hear how a terrible chaperone and grandmother I am!"

"Grandmother, I'm not with child, Cayden and I fell in love, and we wish to be married." She struggled in her arms, but it was useless. "Grandmother!!!"

"Listen to me, Rosemary." She was released when they arrived in the foyer. Like prey facing a predator, Rosemary cowered with fear at her grandmother's reproving glare. "I am done playing these cat and mouse games with you, everyone's aware of your disappearances at Balls and other events—"

"I was only writing," she said meekly.

"They don't know that! What they do think they know is that you were probably with a gentleman. If you are with child, I plan to prove one way or another with the doctor."

At this, Rosemary gasped. Her grandmother didn't trust her, and a crease formed on her forehead.

"It would only prove the rumours true and ruin the family name!"

"I see this is all about your reputation. I care not for what others think of me. Let your doctor come, so I may prove my innocence and show how little you think of me and Lord Knights!"

"Rosemary! How dare you speak to me like that! Come back here!"

But she had already reached the top of the stairs and didn't stop until arriving at her bedchamber.

HE WAS INDEED A coward. Cayden stared at the untouched bottle and glass of whiskey on the table. Drinking always made him remember Eric. A very dark humour his mind played on him, for he knew of persons who drank and forgot. However, he drank and remembered. Drinking also made him sleepy. Too much drinking made him forget for a while, but he always remembered after a few days. His life was complicated. Why on earth had he entered this gentleman's club tonight?

To catch a glimpse of his friend, Jude.

He missed Jude and didn't like this tension between them. He shouldn't have reacted as he did days ago in Jude's study. Instead of visiting and apologizing the following day, Cayden let his stubbornness get the best of him. What he said about using this marriage of convenience as a sort of amusement was wrong. Revealing his plan to die to the man that saved his life was wrong.

Everything was wrong.

Cayden shook his head and was about to leave when he saw Jude entering with the Marquess in tow. Jude's eyes caught Cayden's immediately and a grim expression washed over his face, but he didn't look away. He walked towards Cayden.

"Caswell," Jude greeted curtly, his eyes drifting to the contents on the table. He knew of his drinking habits or better yet, lack thereof and a frown of disappointment appeared.

"Cayden!" the Marquess exclaimed. "What a coincidence meeting you here. Is it not Jude?"

"Yes, I dare say it is." Jude's voice held curiosity.

The Marquess took a seat and quickly poured himself a glass. "Only a half glass at a time. I'm testing myself to be sober at your wedding, Cayden." He grinned, leaning back in the chair, the glass nestled in his palms.

"I'm proud of you." Cayden smiled genuinely. The Marquess was looking rather well, better than he had in months. His beard was shaved, dark hair cut neatly, and his brown eyes now twinkled. Perhaps one good thing was coming out of this wedding after all, Cayden mused. "You look very dashing, it's very suiting."

"He's been trying his best. Even, Kimber, his old nursemaid thinks so too. She even wept when she saw him," Jude said.

The Marquess made a disapproving noise but remained silent.

"Please have a seat, Jude. I wish to speak with you," Cayden pleaded, then exhaled the breath he was holding as Jude took the other seat beside him. "I-I would like to apologize for—"

"No need, I was out of line and should have supported you, if it's what you wished," Jude said.

Cayden frowned at his friend. He wasn't pleased that Jude had agreed, even if that was what he wanted. He'd strangely wanted Jude to fight against it more.

"Caswell! You young devil! When were you going to tell me about your nuptials?" The three occupants at the table groaned in anguish as Lord Bernard, third son of the Earl of Lunrey and information seeker came to stand before them.

"Lord Bernard, what a pleasant surprise," Cayden said dryly. "Came straight to the source of information as always. You put London's famous gossip, Lady Olivia, to shame."

"You know me too well." Lord Bernard smiled crookedly, pulling a seat from the nearby table that was about to be occupied, causing the gentleman to fall on his buttocks. Lord Bernard ignored the curses and planted himself firmly on the seat. "Caswell, rumours are that you got yourself entangled. Who's the unfortunate lady?"

Cayden leaned back, astonished. "Who has been spreading these rumours? It's supposed to be a secret."

"God-dammed!" Lord Bernard, slapped his hands on the table, rattling the liquor and eliciting the Marquess' protest. "I just lost a huge sum of money to your brother. I didn't believe it at first."

Of course, leave it to his brother to get the rumour mill stirring.

"This is... amazing, you got to tell me this lady's name," Lord Bernard said.

Cayden quirked one brow. "I suppose there's a bet on that here too?"

Lord Bernard grew silent for a moment. "If...I'll split the money with you, if you want."

This is unbelievable!

"How much is it?" Jude asked, seemingly interested.

Cayden looked at Jude, like he was utterly mad. "Jude—"

"Ten thousand pounds," Lord Bernard announced, attention fully on Jude now.

"We would take half—"

"Two-thirds."

Cayden watched, dumbfounded at the exchange.

Jude shook his head. "Half and I need Fairy, the pony."

"What the hell do you need a pony for, Jude?" Cayden exclaimed. He could have been dead, and the gentlemen wouldn't budge, for none of them gave him any acknowledgment.

Lord Bernard looked confused. "My little sister's pony? She won that at a fair six months ago."

"You know she cheated Miss Penelope's sister. With the other half of the money, you can buy her another one and have extra for other expenses, not to mention the privilege to gloat about your winnings."

Cayden had heard about that incident, which entailed a lot of crying and humiliation at not winning a pony. He'd been so upset that the little girl didn't win the Pony that he had thought to buy one for her, but it had slipped his mind. If Jude had mentioned it again, he would have done it. This was much better, getting revenge and making a wrong, right.

"What do you say?" Jude spread his arms wide. "There's nothing to lose. Everyone wins in the end."

"Careful Jude, your father's showing," Lord Bernard sneered.

Jude merely shrugged. "Your choice," he replied.

"Fine," Lord Bernard growled. "You have a deal." He turned to Cayden expectantly.

"Her name's Rosemary."

"That's it?' Lord Bernard asked, looking perplexed.

That's all I know. Cayden wanted to say.

"How the devil am I supposed to be satisfied with an incomplete name? Rosemary? A damn herb? Are you jesting Caswell?"

Cayden shook his head, smirking. "Never."

Lord Bernard sighed and drew his blond brows together as he thought for a second.

"Careful Bernard, you'll split your head open if you think any harder." The Marquess grinned over his second half glass. "The lass's name is Rosemary, and she's a dark-haired maiden with green eyes. She's also the one that proposed to him. That should tell you that the lady's got enough attitude to keep Caswell on his toes."

Cayden wished at that very moment that he would pass out.

Jude rested his elbow on the table, covering his face with a palm and Lord Bernard looked as if he had seen Father Christmas.

"She proposed to him!" A broad smile stretched across Lord Bernard's face and the Marquess, who seemed to realize what he had done, pressed his lips together and looked at Jude and Cayden, nervously.

"Well...well..." Cayden looked up to see his brother, smirking down at them. "If it isn't the drunkard, the saint, the corpse and the gossiper. All at one table. Don't see that every day. I didn't miss a meeting, did I?" And to Cayden's horror, Hugh grabbed a chair and joined them.

"This table's getting too crowded," Jude mumbled loud enough for Cayden to hear, and he couldn't have agreed more.

"Tell me, brother. This mysterious engagement of yours, is it still commencing? It has been how many days now without a bride?" Hugh gave him a lopsided grin. "If there is any."

"I am getting married Hugh. She's real," Cayden said. "In a couple of days, I'll be meeting her parents."

Hugh snickered.

"I found out her name and I'll be collecting my money from you and the others," Lord Bernard interposed.

"You, don't say," Huge exclaimed with humour, turning to Bernard. "What is it?"

"Rosemary."

Cayden sighed, watching his brother waiting for more. "That's all there is, brother, for now."

Hugh started to roar with laughter, drawing attention from people in the club. "You—you are indeed a jester, Cayden. No one's even taking you seriously."

"Says the man, whose entire life's been nothing but a joke," the Marquess sneered. It was no secret that Randolph despised Hugh. Cayden didn't know what brought about such loathing, only that it had been there ever since he could remember.

Hugh's eyes narrowed, and he looked at the Marquess with new interest. "You look...decent." Hugh said with much disgust. And Lord Bernard agreed with a nod of a head. "Don't tell me you are still fighting to breathe the same air as I am? Your cousin will be most pleased to hear about this," he said, sarcastically.

The Marquess' cousin was a scoundrel. His attempt to get his hands on the title was endless, but he had been quiet of late, and speculations were that he was waiting until Randolph, withered away in his liquor. If he saw the Marquess now, he would be furious, certainly not pleased.

"It never surprises me that you two are acquainted. After all, you both have the same desires," the Marquess replied.

Hugh's eyes darkened at the Marquess words. Jude stood abruptly, and Lord Bernard scurried away, mumbling something about looking for his money.

"Randolph, I think it's time to call it a night," Jude said, a hand on the Marquess' shoulder.

Cayden was thinking about leaving as well, if only to escape further bickering between his brother and the Marquess. He'd pay Jude a visit tomorrow, as they still had much to discuss after the interruptions they received this evening.

"Yes, Ranny, you better listen to your nursemaid," Hugh taunted. "From the looks of it, he seems to be doing a better job than your mother."

That was all it took to close the club for the night. Chaos erupted.

Chapter Seven

C AYDEN HAD NEVER FELT such a throbbing headache.

One booted foot rested on the armchair, while he sat on another of his mother's favourite armchairs, nursing a swollen eye. The warm cloth the maid had supplied from the kitchen somewhat helped. He frowned. It could have been worse.

Last night was still much of a blur. He didn't remember who had hit him, as everyone started fighting each other. Someone had tried to stop the fight. And the Marquess had punched that person in the face too. the man had gone to punch the Marquess, Jude interrupted, someone tried to hit Jude from behind, Cayden had picked up a chair and knocked the man flat on his face.

Cayden groaned, he did remember how the brawl had started and Hugh's cries of anguish at Marquess's wrath. Hugh had a broken rib, both eyes blackened to the point that they swelled closed and a sprained ankle. That was the description the doctor revealed mere hours ago. If only Hugh had kept his mouth shut and not provoked the slightly drunken Marquess. But this was his brother he was talking about, and Hugh was never one to act sensibly. As always Cayden was caught in the middle of his brother's mess.

He was livid!

A quiet night at the club with his friends and making amends with Jude had turned utterly chaotic! Not only was he injured and miserable, but Cayden along with his friends had been forbidden from entering the club ever again.

Damn you, Hugh!

He made an exasperated noise, shifting his other foot to join the first on the armchair. He was just making himself comfortable, sulking back in the chair, when the drawing room door flew open. Cayden sprung to his feet, kicking the chair backwards, fearing that it was his mother. Lady Caswell would go insane if she saw his feet on her armchair. He grimaced both from the pain in his leg, head, and the realization that it was just Louness, the butler.

"A letter for you, sir!"

The words echoed inside his head.

The pounding in his head increased after that loud announcement. "Thank you, Louness." He tried to muster a genuine smile as he took the letter, but it fell flat. Not that the butler noticed. He continued with his practiced bow and hasty departure.

Cayden frowned down at the letter. Throwing the still warm cloth on a desk nearby, he tore it open. Perhaps it was from Jude? He squinted to read the elegant fine writing. Realizing this wasn't from his best friend, his heart did an unfamiliar leap. "I must be seeing things." Or perhaps his good eye wasn't working properly without the other. With a nervous chuckle, he read it again. And again, until his hands shook, and his head began to hurt and not from the headache.

Rosemary, Richmond, Corbourne, Princess, frogs, blue ,black, purple, green.

He didn't know why he thought of frogs and those colours, but nothing made sense to his brain right now.

His trembling fingers released the letter to tangle in his hair. Rosemary's a princess! A princess proposed to him? This was horrible! He couldn't for the life of him marry a princess. And why the bloody hell did she kept it a secret?

Unable to stand, Cayden dropped back in the armchair, burying his face in his hands. He didn't know whether to scream, cry, or laugh. Of all the possibilities he had thought about as to why she was so secretive about her family, this was not one of them. He couldn't possibly marry her now. Could he? Calling the engagement off would not have been so horrible if only his family had known, not the whole of London! Lord Bernard would waste no time spreading the news of this Mysterious Rosemary who had captured the Earl's heart. Society would weed out every maiden who was named such. It wouldn't be long before they found out who she was. Breaking an engagement to a princess would be madness and ruin the lady's reputation. Doubtless the ruthless King of Blackmane would have his head for bringing disgrace to his family. As much as he wanted to die, Cayden preferred to keep his head attached to his body.

But what if her family found out he was only marrying their daughter because he was bored? And would soon be making her a widow?

Cayden squeezed his eyes shut. He was thinking so much, his head felt like it would explode!

"Cayden darling?" When he didn't lift his head immediately, the footsteps of his mother, flew across the room. "Cayden, are you having a fever?" Dropping on her knees, her hand moved to press his forehead. "Thank heavens!" She breathed with relief . "Do you wish for some more laudanum?"

He sat upright and looked at his mother. "I received a letter from my intended." His mother's face brightened; the sun didn't hold a candle.

"Please, tell me will I be meeting my daughter soon?" She gripped his wrist tightly as if to squeeze the information out of him. For a lady of slender physique, her strength he always marvelled at it. Trusting his son's ability to choose, his mother had already accepted Rosemary as her daughter,. Cayden suspected that since he was his mother's baby, as she always reminded him, he could bring home a toothless old maid and she'd still open her arms to the lady but Rose –Princess Rosemary was no toothless old maid!

"I don't think I can do it, Mother." He shook his head back and forth, glimpsing the frown on her face. "She's—Rosemary..."

"Yes, son, go on, finish the sentence," she said softly, but he heard the demand within her voice. His mother was just as desperate as Lord Bernard and the ton to find out more than just a first name.

"Princess."

"What?" she shrieked.

"Blackmane."

"What?" Her head drew backwards.

"She's a princess, Mother." Her hands slowly slid away from his wrist, and he took that opportunity to stand. "Rosemary Richmond, daughter of the Duke of Corbourne and Princess of Blackmane."

Silence.

It only lasted a second before an excited scream left his mother's lips. "Oh, my Cayden!" She stood and embraced him. "I knew you would marry well, but a princess?" She pulled away slightly and smiled up at him with so much love that tears sprung to both of their eyes. "This is remarkable! I am so proud of you! I knew of a princess making her debut in London, but oh my, I never thought you'd capture her heart. To think, the famous Corbourne family, will be our family! You are marrying into royalty, my love!"

His mother was making him look like a fortune hunter.

"Mother, I didn't know who she was when she—I mean when we got engaged—"

"That's perfect! It means you are not marrying her because of her title." She patted his chest absentmindedly. "Now, tell me when we are to visit?"

Pulling at his cravat, Cayden moved towards the window. The air around him suddenly felt hot.

"Cayden?"

Closing his eyes, he sighed with exasperation. There was no way out of this, and did knowing who she was change anything? No! The plan would still commence. He must marry her, and in a few months leave. It was simple, and no obstacle, especially a mere title, would get in his way.

Nothing will.

With a broad smile, he turned, snatched the letter off the floor, and announced that they would depart for Corbourne Estate two days hence. He couldn't wait to give Rosemary a piece of his mind.

IT WAS TIMES LIKE these Rosemary wished she had socialized more rather than sticking her nose in a book or writing. A female companion was needed to confide in. True, she had cousins from her great uncle Fredrick and Aunt Clarissa, but her cousins were too young to discuss such thoughts of marriage and love. Cayden. Just the name of her mysterious stranger brought a smile to her face. Of course, he was extremely handsome and from a reputable family, but that was not what drew her to him; he was…simple, and she couldn't help noticing a bit of sadness in his expressions.

"Perhaps *simple* wasn't the right choice of words," she whispered, biting her bottom lip as she drifted deep in thought for the right words to describe the man she was going to marry. Cayden didn't stick his nose high in the air like the rest of the aristocrats did. He was down to earth and could be a brute at times. Images of how he tossed her over his shoulder raced through her mind. Was she even thinking that night? Leaning back on the tree trunk, Rosemary brought her knees to rest at her chin. She was so caught up in the urgency of freedom from her grandmother and parents that she grasped the first idea that came to mind without even considering the most important attribute of marriage.

Love.

Her grandmother had scolded her about that, once she finally got over the news that Rosemary wasn't with child. Rosemary had told her grandmother endless times that she wasn't, and it had taken a visit from the doctor for the lady not to storm over to Caswell. Oh what a scene that would have caused, although it would have probably explained the hasty proposal. No one would believe they fell hopelessly in love in such a short time. Her family wasn't convinced, and they looked at her like she was an open book, and they knew the truth.

"It's not like I am trying to please everyone," she grumbled, standing. With a quick shake of her gown, she started to pace. "I am doing this for myself… finally taking control of my life. Love has nothing to do with it. A lot of people marry without it. I don't need it."

She stopped, lifting her gaze to the sky. Rosemary closed her eyes, drinking in the warmth of the sun. She was overthinking again. Taking several deep breaths, she started to walk back to the manor when some bushes rattled as she swept by. She paused for a second and took a step back, eyes widening. She found a stick and waited for whatever creature was behind it. A scream caught in her throat and her hands lifted to strike whatever it was, when red curls sprung from between the bushes, followed by a tiny squeal. Rosemary rolled her eyes, throwing the stick away, her arms folded as she glared down at her little sister.

"Ruby! What are you doing here?"

Innocent blue eyes like their father's stared up at her. "Rosie, I came as soon as I could when I found you missing."

Didn't she realize she wanted to be alone and that she was hiding from her?

"You are worse than the guards, Ruby. I told you not to follow me," she scolded.

"But I must. Grandmother told me that I should act as your chaperone," Ruby said sternly, crawling on her knees.

Rosemary gaped. Grandmother was asking a child of seven summers to watch over her? Oh, the insult! Her hands balled in a fist.

"She told me, that it would keep you out of trouble."

Ruby cocked her head. "Rosie? Are you going to have a baby?"

"No!" The horror! This was worse than the interrogation her mother had given her a few days ago.

"But I heard Grand--"

"How many times have you been warned not to listen at doors?"

Ruby's face turned crimson as she stood. Rosemary shook her head and continued toward the manor.

"Rosie." Tiny footsteps trailed behind her. "Are you getting married?"

"Yes," she replied.

Ruby raced in front of her, causing her to stop. "Will there be a wedding with cake?"

"Of course, silly," She said, placing her hands on her hips. "What's a wedding without a cake?"

"A funeral."

At her sister's blunt remark, Rosemary grinned.

"There was no cake at cousin Sam's funeral," Ruby continued, looking more disappointed about the cake than their distant dead cousin.

"Indeed." She bent her knees slightly and tapped her sister on her tiny, adorable nose, causing her to smile. "It's a good thing I'm having a wedding."

They commenced walking, Ruby humming merrily beside her. "Will there be lots and lots of sweets?" she asked, stopping to look up at her. "Pies! Tarts! More cakes!"

With defeated shoulders, Rosemary looked at her sister wryly. "Lots of it."

"Oh goodness!" Ruby rocked from one foot to the next. "I can't wait!"

Rosemary smiled, watching her sister race back to the manor. "So much for chaperoning."

Chapter Eight

C AYDEN AND HIS FAMILY arrived at the Corbourne Estate just before dawn in the evening. It was the action of desperation to travel at such an hour and in such weather. Cayden had only complied to stop his mother's fussing. There was also a level of anxiousness on his part. In his heart, he was anticipating this visit just as much. He stepped down from the carriage, grimacing as his boots landed in a puddle of water.

"Oh, this is so exciting!" Lady Caswell's eyes were fixed upon the exquisite manor when she took his hand and stepped down from the carriage. His eyebrows rose when his mother walked gracefully up the steps, dismissing any thoughts about the ruining of her gown that swept the water. "Come along, Cayden, we must hurry, it will be pouring soon."

"You do know I made the journey as well?" Hugh grumbled, stepping from the carriage. His eyes were still partially swollen, and he was still in a foul mood but just like his mother, his brother was eager to see Cayden's bride, or was it that he still didn't believe all that he was told? Hugh didn't take the news of his bride's identity very well. Anger was not the word to describe the tantrum his brother had thrown. Hugh had screamed in disbelief, kicked a few chairs, and asked to be left alone in his bedchamber.

Hugh was jealous. But what Cayden's brother didn't know was that there was nothing to be jealous of. That all changed when the door swung open. The butler did not greet them from the other side, but Rosemary. She was breathtaking! Dark tresses swept upwards in a bun, exposing her long slender neck, while her green eyes sparkled like gems caught in the sun and held no competition to the dress she wore of the same colour. Yes, any man would be jealous, indeed. He needed to acknowledge that.

"Oh, Lord Caswell, Lady Caswell and..." She hesitated at Hugh before bestowing another curtsy. "Lord Caswell... please come in. I am afraid we weren't expecting you all to travel in such weather." She closed the door on a soft chuckle, one that Cayden detected as being nervous.

"We always follow through on an invite, dear," his mother said with a broad smile and, as if she couldn't contain herself anymore, she startled them all by embracing Rosemary. "Oh, you are just as lovely as I had imagined! My son, is very fortunate."

Hugh snorted and Rosemary, still blushing, glanced his way before turning to finally look at Cayden. "I – "

"Your Highness!" They all turned to meet an old man, whom Cayden suspect was the butler, advancing towards them. "A lady of the house, shouldn't have to answer her own door."

"It was no trouble at all, Alfred. I saw the carriage through my window and came immediately." She reassured him with a smile. "Please show the guests to the drawing room, and I'll inform my parents of our visitors." She was gone within a second, racing up the staircase, causing his mother to raise her eyebrows in surprise.

"I know that look, Lady Caswell, and you'll find out soon enough how very non-traditional and down to earth they are," the butler announced, gesturing for them to follow.

His mother gave him a smug look. "I believe the more I know about her, the more I'm falling in love."

At that statement, Cayden frowned.

The rain started to pour as soon as they arrived in the drawing room, refreshments were brought, and his mother was occupied with a cup of tea and cakes, while Cayden was much like his brother, staring at nothing in particular when the drawing room door burst open and several individuals hurried inside.

Cayden stood abruptly, his mother and brother following. They curtseyed and bowed respectively. He only recognized Rosemary's grandmother and his bride out of the group, but it wasn't difficult to know who her mother was.

"It's a pleasure to meet finally meet the Caswells." The red-haired beauty greeted them with a smile, her eyes like Rosemary's, shining with excitement. The gentlemen beside her did not smile. In fact, they were practically glaring.

"Why did you make the journey in such a weather?" The gentleman beside her asked with a lifted brow. "We would have understood, but then again, what can I expect from a man who didn't have the courtesy to speak to me before proposing to my daughter?"

"Damien stop it! Our daughter chooses him," the red-haired lady exclaimed, glaring at her husband.

"Papa!" Rosemary stepped forward. "I told you, it was not planned, and it was only my persuasion that caused Lord Caswell to act with such haste!"

"Son. I told you she was with child!" The grandmother's exclamation caused Cayden to gasp in horror. "Why else would there be such a rush?"

Rosemary grabbed hold of her father's arm, halting him from probably beating him to a pulp. "Father, I am not with child. There's haste for this wedding because..." She gazed at Cayden, giving him a sweet coy smile before looking up at her father. "We are in love, Father, and want to get married immediately," she said, releasing her hold on him.

"Love?" Her father frowned. "I thought you barely knew the gentleman."

"No Father," She lowered her gaze to stare at her now entwined fingers. "We have been communicating through letters and at the Balls, that's why I have been brushing off suitors Grandmamma introduced me to."

This lady needed her own stage. She managed to play the innocent, shy, love-struck lady well. Cayden's jaw clenched. His urge to be pleased conflicted with anger. And what was this about being with child? He folded his arms. Such fickle-minded society, whose only explanation for having a hasty marriage was because the lady had been ravished.

"Father, please." Green eyes shimmered with tears. "Lord Caswell's an honourable man; he even served in the king's army."

A sigh left her father's mouth, and his hand rested on Rosemary's cheek before a smile graced his face. "Very well. If it's what you wish." They embraced and, as soon as they parted, Rosemary came to stand beside Cayden. "But I'll have to speak to the young man we have much to discuss."

She nodded and looked up at him with a reassuring smile.

THE RAIN HAD NOT STOPPED. At the Richmonds' hospitality, they were given rooms to stay for the night. Cayden sat in the darkness, staring at the streaks of lightening that flowed through the drapes. *What the hell am I doing?* he asked for the millionth time. Would this all be worth it? But what was *it?* Marrying a princess and receiving higher ranks in society. More wealth, houses, lands... He swept a hand over his face.

Telling more lies?

God, he felt like a fortune hunter. He was the only person gaining from this marriage. All Rosemary wanted was her freedom, freedom to blasted write! Cayden shook his head. He was the guilty one, guilty of the deception, of giving Rosemary less than she deserved. But it was her idea, and she seemed to be excited, unworried. In fact, she was anticipating the marriage.

A light knock at the door was followed by the butler's voice. "Lord Caswell, dinner will be served shortly."

Already dressed, he stood, then taking a deep breath, he left his chamber. Cayden stopped as he closed the door behind him, and his eyebrows lifted. "Your Highness, what are you doing here?"

She gave him a sweet smile. "I came because it's customary for my soon-to-be husband to escort me to dinner."

"I wouldn't have thought you'd be one to stick to traditions."

She blushed and looked away then turned back to stare at him with a grin. "Some traditions are still worth keeping."

"Indeed. I always thought traditions cause for boring storytelling by the way." He smiled.

"In that case, we'll certainly not be without stories to tell our---" Her eyes widened. "Oh my –I didn't mean--"

Cayden remained calm even though his heart felt like it would explode. She was going to say children—he would bet an arm on it. Fear struck him—fear at the thought of having a family with her didn't frighten him. True, he had dreamed of having children but that was before Eric's death.

"Your Highness, we need to talk."

"I-I apologize my lord, sometimes I don't think before I speak and--" She looked like she was about to cry.

Cayden was not thinking either, as he pulled her towards him and crushed his lips to hers. Her lips were warm and soft. She hesitated at first, and he waited until the shock passed. It didn't take long for her to return his kiss and his hands cupped her face as he deepened the kiss. His heart pounded; his mind went blank at the sensations in his body at having her so near.

He pushed her against the door and just as he moved his hands slowly up from her rib cage to her breast, she shrieked and pushed him away. They stared at each other in shock and horror, breathing laboured. Cayden ran his hands through his hair and looked away. What caused him to act so impulsively? He turned back to her, realizing that it was everything about her.

"I-I think I'll just--" And she ran.

Cayden was left miserable at the table when she didn't appear for dinner, sending word she was not well. How the hell was he going to keep her away from him when they were married?

Chapter Nine

OSEMARY HAD NEVER BEEN kissed. But she was certain that no one could compete with Cayden's skills. Her skin still tingled at just the remembrance of it, and she frowned. This was to be a marriage of convenience, certainly that didn't entail feeling this way about one's soon-to-be husband. It would only complicate things. She didn't sleep last night, and it was all his fault. She couldn't even write! A damned permanent distraction. "The cad!"

"Your Highness?" She stared at her lady's maid in the mirror, who was fastening the lace of her corset. "Is it too tight?"

The girl took her outburst as a protest of her administrations. Rosemary sighed. "It's just about right. Are you not finished?"

She nodded and tied the string into a knot before rushing for the beige gown on the bed.

Rosemary didn't know how she would face Cayden this morning after she ran from him like a coward. He would not mock or laugh at her; he was too humble. What he would do was keep quiet and not address it, and Rosemary planned to do the same. As she stepped into the gown, she heard talking in the garden. Quickly, she dressed and moved towards her balcony. There, she saw Ruby and Lord Caswell sitting on the ground having a conversation. Or more likely, her sister was doing most of the talking.

"Grandmama, thought Rosie was with child, and I am acting as her chaperone."

Rosemary's eyes widened. She needed to stop her sister. Who knew what else she had revealed to Cayden. Gathering her gown, she ran from the balcony, down the stairs, and made it outside just in time for Ruby's broken knee story.

"Ruby, you are up early." Ignoring Cayden's gaze, Rosemary smiled at her sister. "I heard Cook's making strawberry eclairs."

Ruby stood and turned to Cayden. "I'll bring some for you, Cayden. Cook makes the best eclairs!"

As she made it out of sight, Rosemary turned to Cayden who had an amused smile on his face.

"Tell me, what you have heard?" Folding her hands, she quirked an eyebrow at him.

"Nothing I didn't witness for myself."

"And just what is that?"

He irritated her even more when he took his time getting to his feet. "Well, you're a liar."

"And you are a saint?"

"I'm not without faults, Your Highness. Please have a stroll around the garden with me." She took his arm gingerly. "We have much to talk about, but first, why did you not tell me who you are?"

❧✦❧

HE PAUSED TO GLARE down at her. Her emerald eyes sparkled under the bright morning sun, and he looked away remembering the kiss, last night. Cayden didn't sleep, couldn't. He had never acted without thinking. He was a soldier, trained to think strategically. Impulsive behaviour was prohibited.

"I don't know what your problem is, my lord. I thought you would be pleased to marry a princess." She shrugged, a smile suddenly playing across her lips. "Or are you intimidated by my family?"

He gave her a murderous look.

"You find humour in this?" He pointed a finger in her direction. "Do you know that I wanted to cancel this engagement?"

A gasp escaped her, and she yanked her hand from his. "You can't!"

"I can!"

"You gave me your word." Rosemary planted her hands on her hips, in a challenging manner.

He exhaled, with a peeved noise. "That was before I knew your family."

"Oh, my faith in war heroes has suddenly been crushed!" she told him. "To think you have dodged bullets and now fear my --"

"I'm not a war hero!" He wished everyone would stop calling him that. "The true heroes are all dead."

Rosemary folded her arms, evidently not discouraged by his shouts. "It would certainly explain your behaviour."

He full on glared at her.

Rosemary grinned. "Your mother seems delighted."

He didn't say anything.

"We should discuss the wedding night."

Cayden frowned.

"It's not something one discuss with one's betrothed. It's not ladylike," he said acidly. "But you've never acted like a lady since I have known you. So, what do you want to know?" He sat on the lawn, stretched his legs.

"I was merely trying to get your attention!"

"You have succeeded," he said, gesturing with a wave of his hand for her to sit.

"Now the wedding night--" he began, and she blushed, playing absentmindedly at the fabric of her gown. What compelled her to speak of such a topic in the first place?

"--There, won't be any," he finished, just as she confessed that she would be delighted to have him.

They both stared at each other in shock.

"What I meant was I would be delighted not to have you," she corrected. "When I blush, my brain lost its senses – You brute!" Cayden couldn't surpress the laughter that rose from his chest, he fell back on the lawn.

"You imbecile!" His laughter turned into howls when he felt her heel make contact with his foot, his injured foot. "Dammit," he cursed. Grabbing a fistful of her gown as she tried to flee, he pulled her back towards him and groaned when her buttocks contacted his chest.

"Let go of me! Arggghh!" She struggled against him, and he flipped her off his chest where she fell backwards on the lawn. "Ouch!" she yelled. He sat upright rubbing at his chest, then met her furious gaze.

"You are heavier than I thought. I might have to ask one of the guards to assist me with carrying you over the threshold--"

"You keep being a boor, and I might strangle you before we wed!" she growled.

"Is that a threat, Your Highness?" He smirked.

"Cayden!" A voice called out in the distance.

Someone was coming.

Rosemary gasped, raising herself on her elbows. Before she could scramble to her feet, Cayden's lips came crashing down on hers. Shocked, she dropped back on the ground, his lips never leaving hers. The kiss started out gentle, as if he was afraid to hurt her somehow or couldn't imagine he was kissing her again. It was like they were kissing for the first time. It then became wild and demanding. She parted her lips on a gasp as his hand pressed just beneath her breast.

Rosemary forgot about the person who was approaching; she wrapped her arms around his neck, wanting to feel his strong physique against her.

"Cayden Knights!"

It was his mother.

"Rosemary!

No, their mothers.

He pulled away and Rosemary whimpered at the loss. She finally opened her eyes, feeling his intense gaze.

"W-why--" Rosemary stuttered.

"We shall be wed before the week is through," he said, hoarsely. "Because heaven knows, I might not go through with it, if we wait any longer."

Realization dawned on Rosemary, and she pressed her lips together to avoid screaming. Everything he'd done was a show for their mothers, and not because he really wanted to. Her arms dropped back to her side, and she turn away from him to stare at Lady Caswell and her own mother's shocked faces.

Chapter Ten

*C*AYDEN WAS RIGHT. They were given five days to prepare for the wedding. Rosemary sat at the long empty table in Blackmane Castle. They had been sent to Blackmane the day after the incident, and it was her wedding night, a night she should feel joyous. She should be laughing like her cousins and friends. Instead, she was in a melancholy state. Her brother, Richard, wasn't present at her wedding and that crushed her very soul more than the fact that the Somersets, her Aunt Clarissa and her family, also weren't here. She missed Richard terribly, it was so unfair that he must be so far from his family—from her—due to the responsibilities of the crown he would inherit soon.

It took her a few years to become aware of the reasons why her parents had her spend as much time as possible with her brother when they were younger. Rosemary's gaze drifted to where Ruby was dancing with Cayden. She smiled as her sister did a clumsy curtsy to commence the dance. Cayden look enchanted by her sister's lively personality. Ruby never got the opportunity to build a relationship with Richard, though her sister had many years to press for one. But Rosemary knew it was not possible. When Richard did return, he would be caught up with duties and work. The king of Blackmane would not die peacefully without knowing if the kingdom was in perfect hands. She hoped Richard was different from her great-uncle, who was indeed ruthless, but kind and dedicated to his family. Her grandfather had told her that the crown made him that way, that it was trying to rule a kingdom like Blackmane and what the king lacked in physical strength, he made up for in intelligence and honesty.

But he never married.

And she hoped Richard didn't share the same fate or allow the crown to change him. She must pen another letter to her brother, soon even though the response was painfully long to arrive, she knew they would put a smile on his face and warm his heart and she was eager to know his thoughts about Cayden.

She spotted the king conversing with her mother. He was not pleased about the marriage. Instead, he had been adamant about making a match with some prince from another country, she couldn't remember the name. Not that she took any interest in entertaining the idea.

"That's not the kind of expression a bride should have on her wedding night."

She pivoted her head, smiling at one of Cayden's friends, Jude Yale, she recalled.

He took a seat. "Do I need to have a word with Cayden?"

"Oh, that will not be necessary. It's my brother—I do wish he was here," she said earnestly.

"Ahh...the young prince. Haven't heard much about him until tonight," Jude said with a smile one could consider as mischievous and admiring.

Rosemary's own lips twitched. "Oh, and what have you heard, Mr Yale?"

"Now where should I start?" At this, Rosemary twisted in the chair to face him properly as he leaned forward in his seat. "Well, the both of you shared a womb, and he's deviously handsome, which doesn't surprise me, for your parents are astonishing."

Rosemary laughed. "I suppose you heard the last bit from the company of the ladies, and indeed he is, but what they forget to mention is that my brother's a terrible tease and can be quite protective. It pains him to be apart from his sisters where he cannot watch us like a hawk."

"I seem to like him already." Jude sat upright, then grabbing a pastry from the table, he stood.

"Where are you off to so abruptly?" She quirked an eyebrow at him.

"Your husband's staring at me murderously, and he's on his way over here this moment."

Rosemary turned to see that it was indeed true. Cayden was no longer dancing with Ruby and was scowling at Jude. As he approached, it gave her the opportunity to stare without him being aware. No gentleman at the ceremony could hold a candle to the man she selected to marry. Cayden was simply beautiful. His blond hair, although she would have liked it to remain long, was cut skilfully, with a few curls falling over his forehead. Her gaze travelled down to his broad shoulders that filled out the dark waistcoat. She dared to go further, and a blush heated her cheeks when she remembered how those arms had held her as they had kissed during the church ceremony. It wasn't like the previous two they shared; it was chaste but still sent her heart fluttering.

"Jude, I hope you haven't spoken ill of me in my wife's presence?" He stopped and looked down at her with a soft smile that made her head spin. *His wife...* the way he said it with so much affection. Rosemary inhaled deeply. And had to remind herself that this was all for show. He didn't love her. He wouldn't even touch her tonight. He had said as much.

"We haven't got to that part," Jude replied, laughter in his voice.

Cayden looked at his friend once more, then with a tiny shake of his head returned his gaze to her. "Do you wish to dance, my dear?"

Graciously, she took his arm, and he led her to the dance floor. He held her close to him for the waltz, making it aware to everyone that they were indeed married. She closed her eyes, savouring being in his arms, if only for this moment.

"Rosemary? Why are you so quiet? I apologize for my absence—"

"What for?" Her head snapped up to stare into bold blue eyes. "I adore you dancing with my sister. She was very excited. I should be the one to thank you." She smiled and he quickly looked away. A pang of hurt coursed through her heart, and her smile slipped. She wanted to cry. He was sweet and lovable around others but alone—he was cold and distant.

She inhaled a deep breath and kept the smile on her face. She was a Richmond and would not cry on her wedding night. Besides, this was a marriage of convenience, she reminded herself. A fact too easy to forget whenever he was near.

"I'm getting tired. Should we not be on our way?" she asked.

She felt him stiffen and he nodded at her. "Very well." He ushered her off of the dance floor and, as they said farewell to their parents, she couldn't wait to be alone with her thoughts. They were going to one of her family's larger cottages not far from the castle to spend a couple of days before returning to one of Cayden's homes in the countryside. She didn't mind at all that she'd be living with other persons. Her husband's mother was a sweetheart and his brother—well, she didn't want to further spoil her night thinking of him.

Rosemary was the first to enter the carriage and with a long sigh, one by one she slipped the gloves off her hands. Her eyes landed on the huge stone on her finger that Cayden had placed on it earlier.

"We must make haste," Cayden mumbled to the footman as he climbed into the carriage. Rosemary lay the gloves on her lap and stared out the window as the carriage took off. He was rushing to be rid of her as quickly as possible. She was glad for the comforting darkness of the carriage, which hid her tears.

"You should be pleased. You got what you wanted. We are finally married, and you can write continuously. I won't object," he said with a hint of laughter.

"I am," she replied, curtly. "And don't you dare mock me. It might be silly to you--"

His hands lift in surrender. "My apologies, no need to get upset on your wedding night."

She didn't say anything until they reached the cottage. "I'm going to my chamber." Not waiting for the footman to fully open the door, Rosemary flew out of the carriage.

CAYDEN FROWNED WATCHING ROSEMARY storm into the magnificent house. It was theirs; the king had given it to them as a wedding present, even after he said honestly that he wanted Rosemary to marry a prince. Cayden couldn't ponder on the decor as he strode to catch up with his wife.

As she took two steps at a time, she lifted the gown, which had made his breath catch during the ceremony. She was radiant, showing that she had been here many times before by the way she easily maneuvered through the halls.

"Rosemary wait!"

She disappeared behind a door, and he followed. "What has gotten into you? I was to carry you over the threshold."

"Well, I guess that's one tradition you are keen on upholding tonight." She swung around to face him. "And don't worry about the servants, they won't say a word, my lord."

He stared at her in bewilderment, arms folded. "We agreed to a marriage of convenience, Rosemary... are you...having second thoughts? And I told you there would be no wedding night. It would ruin everything. It's for the best."

She looked away and moved to have a seat on the bed. "I understand." Somehow, he doubted that she did. "Would you excuse me so I can get ready for bed?"

Cayden looked around the chamber and spotted his trunks. "I believe this is our bedchamber. It appears as newlyweds we are to share a chamber... every night." Taking a deep breath, he stared at his angelic wife, whose eyes widened in shock. If this were under different circumstances, she would already be in his arms. But he couldn't. He looked away and went to gather his belongings. "Are you certain about the servants not speaking of this?"

"Yes. But if you are not convinced, you can stay here. I'll-- surely the bed is big enough for two?"

Not big enough to keep him from touching her and, with a shake of his head, Cayden scurried out of the chamber.

THE FOLLOWING MORNING, Rosemary awakened and went to her writing desk. But instead of finishing her book, she began to write in her other journal. Last night she had thought of how empty and fake her wedding was and realized that she didn't want that in a marriage. How foolish was she to think that she would be happy in a marriage without love? Only one thing was on her mind at the time—to escape her family's nagging and being able to do whatever she wanted without hiding in the shadows. So caught up she was, that she forgot about her own happiness. Freedom didn't mean happiness. She wanted more and Cayden had showed her that there was more to marriage with his kisses.

She wanted more.

A soft knock at the door caused her to place her feather quill down and rise to her feet. "Your Highness, breakfast is ready."

"Thank you, please inform my husband that I'll be there shortly."

"I'm sorry, Your Highness, but your husband left early this morning."

Rosemary's heart hammered in her chest. Did he run off just a day after their marriage? "Did he say when he would be back?" She couldn't stop her voice from wobbling.

"No, Your Highness."

At breakfast, Rosemary tried to get some of the delicious food in her stomach as she sat listening for some sort of noise or hooves riding towards the cottage to indicate Cayden's arrival. After she had spent more time that necessary at the breakfast table, she left and resigned to her chamber for the duration of the day. It was late evening when he arrived, and she heard his heavy footsteps sweep past her chamber.

She climbed out of bed and strolled down the hall, then without knocking, she opened the door and slammed it back shut. The words stuck in her throat as Cayden sat shirtless on the bed. His eyes widened at her intrusion and he paused from pulling off his riding boots. "Is anything the matter?"

She intook a deep breath and concentrated on his face. "Where -- were you?"

"I went for a ride around the cottage," he stated.

She paced twice before turning back to him. "I thought you left me." Rosemary blinked back tears and exhaled. "I know I said the servants won't talk of my loveless marriage, but that gave you no right to humiliate and worry me like this!"

"My apologies," Cayden replied dryly, as he continued to take off his boots. "I just needed...some time to think and it's a beautiful place."

"Yes, it is," Rosemary answered. "Perhaps we can take a stroll around the garden or a ride—"

"That won't be necessary." He stood and moved towards her with a frown. Rosemary tried desperately not to show her disappointment. "Besides, I thought you said, you'd be too occupied to do anything, if it doesn't involve a pen or a paper."

"I—do, I am." She stared up at him, and he gave her one of his heart stopping smirks that would render any woman speechless, including her.

"Perfect, I can't wait to read it." He moved past her, disappearing behind the changing screen.

"It's not the sort of thing gentlemen reads."

"Given the fact that I sacrificed my freedom, giving you the opportunity to finish whatever it is you are writing, I can spare some more of my time and read the blasted thing."

"Sacrificed?" Her mouth gaped opened. "When I found you in the garden that night, it looked like you were trapped as much as I was, not to mention miserable."

Cayden groaned. "You made it sound like I am some stray cat you found." When he emerged from the changing screen, he looked very much the same, only the clothes were cleaner. She stared at his white linen shirt and black breeches, then at the clothes on the bed. "What is it?"

"Your attire. It's all the same."

"And?" His eyebrow arched.

She shrugged. "Nothing." He glared at her, and she sighed in defeat. "It's all so dull—"

A knock at his door, had Cayden mumbling a sigh of relief.

Giving him an amused look, she went to open the door.

"Dinner is ready, Your Highness." The young servant said before curtsying and rushing back down the hall.

She turned back to her husband. "Shall we?" She turned once more to leave, when he grabbed hold of her arm, took a step forward.

"I'll escort you. Just because it's a marriage of convenience doesn't mean we would succumb to barbarism. We will maintain decorum."

She nodded. "We should have a list of things that are acceptable and not," she began as they made their way to the dining room.

"I thought we already had?"

"No. I'll write the list and have it to you by morning."

Chapter Eleven

"WHAT DO YOU THINK about the list?" Finding nothing else to look at, Rosemary turned from the carriage's window. The place she had called home disappeared between the trees. She was on her way to a start a new chapter in her life and make a home of her own with her husband. Her very reluctant husband, Cayden, was a very mysterious man, which puzzled her to the extent that she saw it as a challenge. The past three days, he had done nothing but distance himself from her, which shouldn't cause her such dismay for it was what was agreed upon. But it did. She had given up on the fact that she no longer could pretend that she wanted a loveless marriage. She had already lied to her parents, claiming that it was a marriage out of pure love and wanted to turn her lie into the truth.

"I have read parts of it."

He was a terrible liar. She glared at him until he groaned with frustration and dug the letter from his waistcoat pocket. He opened it and she watched for any expression on his face, but none was given.

"Very well—I agree."

"That's it? Are you mocking me Cayden? Surely you have some objections?"

"No, I don't. I said I agree, is that not sufficient?"

"I-I supposed," she stuttered.

"Are you certain you'll be comfortable living with my family?" he asked.

"I am certain."

"And the servants?"

"Yes."

"I can get---" he began, but stopped abruptly when she reached out to touch his hand gently.

"Cayden, tis all right." It was the first time, she'd called him by his name since they married. She stared into his startled expression, before his gaze dropped to where she laid her hand on his. She immediately recoiled and sat back in her seat, feeling the warmth of her cheeks. "I'm sorry."

The rest of the journey was spent with barely any conversation. When they arrived at the Caswell estate, it was nightfall.

"It's not as glamorous as your castle—"

She touched his arm gently, drawing his attention to her. It was a gesture she used instinctively whenever he started to worry. This time, she didn't apologize. "It's perfect..."

He smiled, but it didn't reach his eyes and led her into the hall where everyone was waiting to be introduced. Cayden's mother and brother were still at Blackmane and were due to return in a few days, giving the newly married couple a few days for themselves. After she had met the staff, Cayden left her standing in the hall with one of the servants. Too exhausted from the long journey to protest, Rosemary watched him go with a sigh.

"Don't worry, Your Highness, he's just going to see about the horses—please let me escort you to your chamber," the young maid offered.

Rosemary wordlessly climbed the staircase, her mind too occupied to admire her new home. She turned to the lovely brown eyed girl, whose hair was a mess of tangled dark curls. "Horses? Is it not too late to deal with the horses?"

"Lord Caswell is very fond of horses and one of them is with child. Tis only natural that he's concerned," she replied.

Rosemary nodded and as an idea came into mind, she swiftly grabbed the girl's hand. "What else is my husband fond of?"

The startled girl looked down at their entwined hands, then back at Rosemary. "Your Highness?"

Rosemary, feeling a little embarrassed at her gesture, quickly released the girl. "My apologies, but I wish to know what pleases him? Makes him smile?"

They continued walking, and Rosemary suspected the girl wasn't going to mention anything for fear of being sacked. "What's your name?"

"Beth," she whispered.

"Short for Elizabeth?"

The girl shook her head. "No. It's just Beth."

"Beth, I assure you, whatever you tell me will not get you in trouble. I'm merely trying to get to know my husband."

The girl looked at her quizzically before pushing the door open, and Rosemary entered in awe. It was large and spacious with a four-poster bed that could hold at least three persons. The room was brightened by candlelight and lanterns and most importantly, someone had thought of placing fruit on the bed. She rushed to it and took a fistful of grapes. "This is very thoughtful."

"Lord Caswell enjoys fruits at night."

Rosemary turned to Beth, who stood awkwardly in the middle of the room. Rose stared at her in such a way to intimidate her to say more.

"He-He also likes strawberry cakes—"

Rosemary loved anything sweet and admired horses. So far so good, she thought with a smile.

"He likes sitting in the garden and watching the birds."

She loved nature, birds included.

"He hates pies."

Oh no! She loved pies.

"What kind of pies?" she asked.

"All of them," Beth replied.

With a conspiratorial groan, Rosemary went to the vanity table and took a seat. Guess she'd have to sacrifice pies. Beth came up behind her and started to unpin her hair. "Tell me more." She popped a grape in her mouth, listening attentively as Beth continued telling her the things that Cayden liked and didn't like.

THE NEXT MORNING, ROSEMARY awoke early, groggy and irritable. She wasn't used to waking at such wee hours. Nevertheless, she climbed out of bed, got dressed, and rushed to the kitchen, where she instructed the cook on what to make. She then rushed to the dining hall, arriving just in time to sit at the table before Cayden entered. He was looking handsome as ever in his white linen shirt and dark breeches. She had told him about his dull appearance, which he didn't seem to want to change, except for his tasseled boots.

"Morning, dear wife." He gave her a quick peck on the cheek for their audience at the door, even though the footmen weren't looking. "You are up early."

"Good morning, Cayden, and is that disappointment I hear?" she teased.

He frowned, then looked at the footmen as he took a seat on the opposite side of the table. "Of course not. I just didn't take you for an early riser."

"Oh, I'm always keen to get a head start." She chuckled, removing the lie from her tongue with a sip of water. Cayden was looking at her suspiciously before he gave a dismissive shake of his head.

The first course of their meal came and, as the lid came off the plate, she shrieked with horror. "Oh no! I detest boiled eggs, please remove it and have cook return it scrambled. Thank you."

Cayden's eyebrows rose when she looked at him in dismay. "You detest boil eggs?"

She nodded. "Can't stand them, it looks as if I'm eating a whole chick."

"Hmm..." He sliced his porkloins into exactly five slices. "That's strange, I could have sworn I saw you eat them back in Blackmane." She watched as he placed a slice of pork in his mouth and started chewing, while watching her every move.

She was never one to back down from a challenge and instead of panicking, smiled sweetly at him. "It wasn't really an egg; it was a dessert shaped like an egg." She shrugged, reaching for the water once more, while Cayden almost choked from laughter.

"A- dessert shaped like an egg?" he said, still laughing.

Rosemary gave him a deadpan look. "Yes. It's a tactic to disguise my dessert into healthy food choices and our cook in Blackmane castle was excellent."

He didn't seem to accept her explanation, but didn't press any further, and she exhaled slowly with relief. Soon her eggs returned, and they ate in silence. "Oh!" she exclaimed, rising to her feet,

Cayden stood abruptly as well. "What is it?"

"I have to go feed the horses, If I'm to live here, I should meet the stable animals as well—get acquainted."

"I THOUGHT SHE HAD changed her mind." Cayden said softly combing his hands through his hair. "I knew this was going to happen. I'm just so irresistible." He paused, a smirk lingering on his face as he caught Jude rolling his eyes. "I saw that." He hadn't been sure if Jude was back from Blackmane and had only travelled here hoping to see him. It was such a relief that he was indeed here, and he had someone to speak to.

"I wasn't trying to hide it." Jude leaned back in his seat, eyes narrowing at him. "I believe you are overreacting—perhaps depriving yourself from an actual wedding night with your lovely wife is starting to show its effect."

"No." Cayden shook his head. "You don't understand, she's trying to gain my favours by doing things I'm fond of."

"Or it could be the both of you have something in common and you don't want to admit it."

Cayden pressed his palms on the desk. "Jude, she was shovelling horse shit, this morning."

Jude's lips twitched into a smile.

"She's a princess. I doubt she had ever done it before." Cayden stood upright, pinching the bridge of his nose. "Heavens, if anyone finds out about this, especially the king..."

"You'll be dead, which is what you wanted, isn't it?" Jude stated on a sigh.

"Only on my terms," he mumbled.

"What's a better way to go than by the hands of a very noble, wealthy man and, if you are fortunate, you may be in history books."

Cayden dropped back in one of the chairs. "Why do you mock me? I didn't come to talk about my death but my wife's--" He paused, waving his hands in the air with uncertainty as he tried to find the right words. "Change in behaviour."

Jude sighed, then leaned forward, elbows on the desk. "Your wife is full of many surprises. Cayden, this could all be a coincidence, but if it isn't, why not simply test her endurance? There must be something you like that she loathes."

Cayden eyes widened. "Jude, you are brilliant!"

"Thank you," Jude replied with a smirk.

CAYDEN STARED DOWN AT his wife, who was sleeping peacefully, her dark hair spread around the sheets for she had slid from the pillows. With her mouth half opened, and arms spread wide, and even so dishevelled, he still found her beautiful. If things were different, he would be making love to her at this time. Inhaling deeply, he pushed that thought away and began to shake her.

"Go away." She swatted his hands, turning on her side with her back to him. So much for rising early, he thought amusedly as he shook her again. "Uggggh... what!" she screamed, turning to him with irritation.

"Rise and shine, we've got work to do."

Realization slowly sank in, and she sat upright, bringing the sheets to her chest. "Cay-Cayden? What are you doing here?"

"Why, getting a headstart on the day."

"What?" She looked at the window. "It's still the middle of the night!"

"No, it's not." He frowned.

"Cayden, I can see stars from here." She glared at him. "And why are you dressed in rags?"

"We are going in the stables." He thought he saw a look of disgust on her face, but it was gone before he could be certain, replaced with a smile that looked so forced he wondered if it might crack.

"Oh, how wonderful. I love horses so much., You'll never believe what I was dreaming," she exclaimed.

"It's difficult to think you were dreaming about shovelling horse manure and didn't want to wake from it."

Her face fell. The smile had finally cracked, then she shocked him. "Oh my God, how did you know."

His jaw hung open, as she pushed the covers off her body, swung her feet off the bed, and rushed to the wardrobe. "Cayden, I'll meet you downstairs," she said over her shoulder.

Cayden watched her rampaging through the wardrobe before wordlessly leaving the chamber. She was trying to challenge him; he shouldn't let her get under his skin. He knew she was pretending to like the things he liked. But who told her he liked shovelling horse shit? Once he had done the blasted thing, his admiration of horses had ended there...with just the horses.

She was down the stairs in the next minute, wearing a pink faded gown, with hem high enough to show her stockinged calves. Her hair was placed in a neat coil upon her head, and she wore the widest smile. "Come along, dear husband, the stables await."

With his teeth grinding, he followed. Perhaps it was determination or pride, which had her shovelling with such dedication. It made him wonder if he was wrong. He even started to question himself if this was one of the things he enjoyed doing?

In the stables, he gazed at her, sweat beading from her forehead, arms grabbing the shovel. If he asked to see her palms, they would resemble a tomato. She even looked like she wasn't breathing; if not for the rapid rising of her chest, which had very admirable breasts.

His gaze lingered there for too long, and when he looked up, she was staring at him. "I'm sorry, I must have dozed off a bit."

"In an atmosphere, like this? What, are you drunk?" she asked.

"The strong stench in here is burning my eyes."

"It makes more sense if you just admit that you were staring at my breasts. Although I might be inclined to believe that last excuse." She wiped at her forehead with the back of her hand.

One of the horse's neighed loudly, and they turned towards its stall. Another neigh and they were running towards it, shovels forgotten.

"It's Dew!" Cayden stared in amazement at the animal that was ready to give birth and fast too, for they were already seeing a foot.

"Cayden, what do we do?" she asked incredulously.

"We wait and watch." He took a seat where he stood, and she followed. "You've never seen a horse give birth before, have you?" he asked, not taking his eyes off the animal.

"No. But I have read about it."

Of course.

He stole a glance at her, noticing the pure joy on her face.

"Oh, Cayden look!" She pointed. "It's going to be grey!"

She was right. The foal was already halfway into this world. "Amazing! I don't think I have owned a grey horse before!"

"Come, on you can do it!" she urged, and Cayden silently expressed his own excitement. It looked to be a smooth delivery, and when the foal was out, Rosemary surged to her feet. "Yes!"

Cayden laughed and watched as the foal tried to walk, two tries and it was up. "Dew! You did it!"

He turned to his wife and engulfed her in a tight embrace. Still holding her he spun her twice, earning giggles from her before placing her on the ground. He pulled away slightly. She was grinning at him with flushed cheeks. It was like he had no control of himself. He saw one of his hands palm her cheek, and before he knew it, he was kissing her. It was a soft, gentle kiss, which send his heart throbbing and made him lightheaded. Dew's neighs brought him back to reality, and he broke the kiss. He took a huge step backwards. His back hitting the stable door caused him to stop, and he stared at his wife, who looked just as shocked as he was, but not remorseful.

She looked away, turning to the foal and its mother. "Do- Do you have a name? I was thinking..."

When was she not? Even during that kiss, she was probably thinking, which he couldn't understand. He didn't even realize he had a brain when he was kissing her, and that was dangerous.

"I-I was thinking... oh dear..." She hesitated.

"Your Highness?"

"Beth!"

As Rosemary darted from the stables, Cayden moved out of the way before he was trampled. He heard her telling the girl that they got a foal before the voices disappeared. Cayden slid to the ground, burying his face in his hands. He needed to stop kissing her so impulsively.

"ROSEMARY?"

"Yes?" She looked across the table to find Cayden's mother staring quizzically at her and his brother looking at her with a frown. She didn't dare look at her husband. Thoughts of him had kept her up all night. The kiss was magical and not at all like the others. She was convinced that every time he kissed her it kept getting better and better—different in the most amazing way possible. The one in the stables felt magnificent. Perhaps there was a chance that he might fall in love with her after all. But how could you possibly tell by a kiss?

"You look a little lost, dear," Cayden's mother interrupted her thoughts.

"I'm sorry, I must have been wool-gathering." She felt heat rise to her cheeks, and finally took the fork in her hand.

"About something amusing it seems by the smile you had on your face," Hugh said.

She sensed a hint of irritation in his voice and looked up before stabbing the sausage with her fork.

"It was very pleasing indeed," she retorted. She didn't like Cayden's brother, not only because he didn't smile, or stood in the corner at her wedding scowling at her guests, including his own brother. Rather, it was because he scared her, made her blood churn whenever she was in his presence with his leering dark blue eyes, which looked at her in the most eerie way possible. She turned back to the others. "Did I miss anything important—Cayden, did you tell them about the foal?"

"It's what we were just discussing." He didn't look, at her evidently thinking the glass of orange juice was more worthy.

"Cayden informed me that this was your first birth experience. I hope it didn't scare you from making—"

"Mother! Don't you finish that sentence!" Cayden's head snapped around to gape at his mother.

"Don't worry Lady Caswell, I wasn't scared, nor did it change my mind about certain things." The ladies then exchanged a pleasant, conspiratorial smile. "It was fascinating."

"Oh, how wonderful. You should name it Rosemary."

"No," Cayden said firmly.

"Indeed," she mumbled. Ignoring his protest, she tapped her index finger to her cheek and started to think. "Oh, I've got it! Dove!"

"I will not be calling a horse Dove." Cayden gritted out.

"I like it," his mother said.

Rosemary held his gaze challengingly. "Why not? It's a beautiful name."

"Because Dove is already a name of an animal, you wouldn't call a rabbit, snake, would you? Nor a cow, tiger."

Rosemary's laughed when she pictures a cow with a tiger pattern, not necessarily relating to what he was saying, but it was amusing. "All right, you have made your point. I have another... Mystic."

Cayden took a moment to reply. "Very well. I approve."

She grinned. "Thank you." And the rest of breakfast was spent with Rosemary in total bliss. Cayden had just allowed her to name one of his horses, his favourite animal.

The rest of the day Rosemary secluded herself in the library with her journal, only stopping to eat some of the delicacies Beth brought. She heard the door open and finally looked up from her writing. Outside the sun was getting ready to sleep. She stood, closing her journal with a sigh.

"It's time I get ready for supper, Beth."

"I'd love to assist."

Rosemary eyebrows lifted, and she turned to meet Hugh. "Hugh! I was just leaving." She hugged the journal to her chest, ignoring his inappropriate comment moments ago. It wasn't wise to entertain such conversations. "The library is yours now."

Moving towards the door took her closer to him, and when he gave her the impression that he wasn't going to get out of her way, she stopped.

"Surely we can share," he drawled. "It's a big library."

"I'm finished. Now would you please excuse me?" she said firmly.

"There's no need to fear me, Princess. We are family."

"Then start acting like it. Since I met you, you have been nothing but hostile and cold. You didn't smile once at your brother's wedding, and you look upon his wife in the most disrespectful lewd manner!" Her chest rose with anger.

"Oh, so you have noticed me." He grinned, moving towards her. Every step he took, she took two backwards. "And here I thought everyone was too busy looking at my brother and his gorgeous bride."

Her eyes widened. "You're jealous." A part of her had always known, but what shocked her was his courage to admit it.

"Just tired of him getting all the precious gemstones when I'm left with rocks!" he shouted.

He moved nearer and she stopped, smelling the liquor on his breath, "You are intoxicated, and I'm willing to overlook this behaviour of yours as such and not inform my husband."

"He won't believe you." He smirked. Standing mere inches from her, he leaned to whisper in her ear. "Because he's a foolish excuse of a man."

She lifted her hand, slapping him across the cheek. "Don't you dare speak of my husband like that!"

He started to laugh, rubbing at his cheek. "You've got more guts than him. I think I like you even more."

"You disgust me!" she snarled and walked briskly out of the library. His taunting laughter, followed her. She was furious to the point where she was shaking. She returned to her chamber and slammed the door forcefully.

Beth gasped and rushed towards her. "Your Highness, what's troubled you?"

Rosemary started to pace angrily, the journal swinging from her fingers. She had no other friends to converse with. It was one of the reasons she detested the castle. One of the reasons she wouldn't run to her parents. One word from her and they'd drag her back to Blackmane and possibly torture her husband for not protecting her. They would have his brother killed. She couldn't let such a thing happen; she was getting very fond of Cayden.

"Princess Rosemary?"

She stopped and glared at Beth. "Stop calling me Princess, I have a name - Lady Rosemary Caswell." With an audible sigh, she threw her journal on the bed and turned swiftly back to Beth, who was looking rather solemn. "My apologies, Beth, I'm just not in a good mood."

"No need to apologize, Prin-Lady Rosemary Caswell."

Rosemary pinched the bridge of her nose and looked away, suffocating a smile. "Lady Caswell, will do just fine. Have you seen my husband?"

Beth shook her head. "He went out this evening and has not yet returned."

"He won't miss supper; I'll see him there."

Supper was the worst. Not only did Cayden not make an appearance, Hugh was there smiling at her smugly. Rosemary couldn't finish her desert and pushed it away. His mother seemed to be the only one in high spirits and engaged her in conversations she must know Rosemary wasn't interested in by the way her eyes kept drifting towards the door. She stayed awake the entire night until her eyelids got too heavy awaiting his arrival.

She awoke, wishing that he would be there, staring at her with those shining amazing eyes, ready to take her to the stables. A sad smile grazed her lips as she recalled the previous day. She had never done such manual labour before and couldn't fathom how someone would call such a thing a hobby. Reading, writing, painting—those were hobbies. But her husband was a very strange man; and strange people did things that normal people would call strange. She sighed, sprawling her arms wide as the door opened.

Another day. Another chance.

Beth dressed her quickly, and upon hearing Beth's information that Lord Caswell was still sleeping, she went to her husband's chamber. She used the adjoining door. His bedchamber was larger and very spacious. On the bed, he lay with his face buried in the pillow still wearing the clothes from yesterday.

"Cayden?" She shook him. "Cayden!"

He rolled on his back; his eyes squinted at her. "What-what are you doing in here?" One hand came up to rest on his forehead.

"Where were you yesterday?" She folded her arms and waited. "You missed supper, and I was quite worried." She bit her lips, trying to hold back the question she wanted desperately to ask. It wasn't the sort of thing one asked a gentleman.

"Stop, no one's around for your performance," he spat.

Her mouth hung open, and she snapped it shut, watching as he stood and moved towards the wash basin. He wasn't drunk, and that helped ease the anger brewing within her. "Whether this marriage is fake or not, I am a human, and we get worried when someone we know might be in danger. I wasn't the only one. Your mother was as well, even though she tried to hide it."

He splashed water on his face, sighing with contentment before turning back to look at her. His eyes blazed with fury. "Stop acting like a concerned, nagging wife, and start acting as you promised—being so occupied with your writing that you forget I even exist!"

"You don't seem to be holding up to your bargain either, since you choose to embarrass me before your family. Not showing for supper and coming home at the wee hours just a few days after we married. No one would ever believe that this is a loving marriage."

"Embarrass? Let me tell you something about my family." He took a step forward, and glared down at her. "Hugh doesn't care, and my mother is too blinded by happiness that I'm married to even notice my absence."

"How very wrong you are."

"I have had enough of this." He moved passed her, mumbling, "Barely here a week and already wants to lecture me about my family."

"Were you with another woman?" she blurted, and she watched as his hands hovered over the doorknob and he turned to her, startled. "I need to know if I'm to be made into a laughingstock." She choked on a sob.

His face softened to an almost sad expression. "I was here the entire night. Mystic's not feeling well."

Immediately after Cayden left. Rosemary returned to the stables, and found it was indeed the truth. Mystic was lying on the floor, looking very weak. He lifted his head as if sensing her presence, and she rushed to him. "Oh Mystic, what's wrong?"

She sat and placed the foal's head, in her lap. "Please don't leave us." The foal closed his eyes as she started to smooth its mane. Looking around the stables, she noticed some hay had a dent in it, as if someone had lain there. Her husband had really spent the night here with the animal and it made her felt foolish for ever speaking such a thing aloud, and even thinking that he might be breaking their wedding vows. She sighed and made herself more comfortable by pressing her back against the board. From the other stall, she heard Mystic's mother and tears came to her eyes. She remembered whenever her sister Ruby was in distress, she would usually sing for her and it always soothed her.

Chapter Twelve

A N HOUR LATER, CAYDEN entered the stables to the sounds of a siren. It led him to the stall where he had placed Mystic, separating the foal from his mother. He met his wife sitting with the foal in her lap, smoothing the animal's mane, as she sang to it. Cayden was mesmerized. His wife was full of surprises. He stood there listening to the melody, until she looked up with those huge green misty eyes that shone brighter than any stars in the dark sky. "

"Cayden." She smiled, and his heart did a tiny leap as if startled. Her eyes lowered. "Is that for me or Mystic?"

Dumfounded, he looked down, and stared at the basket like it was the first time, he had ever seen it. "Uh... Yes. Both of you." He shook his head, moving further in the stall. "I brought some milk for Mystic. When I didn't see you at breakfast, I knew where you had gone."

He lowered to his knees and took out the pouch he had Cook poured milk into, it had a small nozzle to force it inside the foal's mouth. Placing it on the ground, he took out the sandwich he had packed. "Here." He extended it for her to take and she shook her head.

"I'm not hungry." She said politely. "Please, may I feed him?"

He solemnly nodded, placed the sandwich back in the basket, and handed her the pouch instead. He watched as she started feeding the foal, squeezing the pouch gently and waiting patiently for it to drink. The foal's drinking was a lot slower than last night. He wasn't aware of the animal's difficulty until his return from riding. It had been a while since he had ridden through his estate, and it was the perfect time to clear his mind from his beautiful wife and the way she felt in his arms.

"What do you think is happening to him?" she asked.

"He's refusing to eat. I already send for the doctor."

"Will he be able to help? Mystic's not like us," she said softly, her hand never stopped soothing the animal.

"I am aware, but Doctor Patello's father was a breeder of horses. I'm depending on his son's experience of watching his father deal with the animals to save Mystic."

"I do hope he survives." She looked up, giving him a sad smile. "And I'm sorry for what I said—"

He lifted a hand in the air, silencing her. "Don't—I gave you every reason to think such. I should be the one apologizing."

They exchanged a smile of acknowledgement before she looked away, focusing back on the foal.

"You sang beautifully."

"I used to sing a lot to my sister, and she enjoys it. You know Ruby, she always speaks her mind and was never pretentious." She finally looked up and grinned at him. "Do you want to hear a story?"

"I don't think I have a choice." Cayden grinned back; it was so easy to get captivated by her.

"Last Christmas, Victoria and Theodore came from Somerset along with their parents, my Aunt Clarissa and Uncle Thomas. You haven't met them yet—they are currently in America visiting my uncle's sister. I have never travelled to that continent before. I've heard it's beautiful and the weather is so different from England—"

Cayden cleared his throat. *My word, if she writes like she speaks, my brain will explode.* "I believe we have a Christmas to discuss."

"Oh, yes—sorry—"

His lips twitched into a smile.

"Victoria and Theodore were spending Christmas with us, and we have this tradition that everyone buys each other a gift but don't write their names on it. So, we don't know who gives who what. Ruby loves receiving presents and Christmas was, of course, her favourite season." She looked at the foal momentary, before continuing. "Ruby was opening one of her presents when she gasped; we all turned to see what she got. It was a bonnet and a green dress, we all thought her exclamation was one of joy, when she said, 'What a horrendous piece of attire! The person who made this should be pricked with the same pin that made this, and this should be burnt!'"

"No," Cayden exclaimed. "That's so blunt and mean."

Rosemary started to laugh. "I thought it hilarious because it was the truth."

Cayden grimaced. "That bad?"

She nodded. "And it wasn't the end. Theodore, looked at his sister, who on the verge of tears, simply said, 'Victoria you had many pin pricks stitching that dress. I guess justice was served after all.' No one else found it amusing, but I did. I didn't stop laughing for the entire day."

"You're terrible." He grinned, and she shrugged nonchalantly.

"Victoria proclaims herself an excellent fashion protege at such a young age, and I would have been more sympathetic, if she wasn't so boastful about it. She even dresses strangely, matching colours that have no business on clothes, but I do love her." She smiled, removing the now empty bottle from the foal's mouth. "Well, would you look at that? He drank it all."

"Indeed," he mumbled. "Here, let me take him." Without waiting for her answer, he took the foal's head, resting it in his lap and stretched his feet. Rosemary, moved then, fishing in the basket, she took out something wrapped in a cloth, and he smirked. *Let's see if you'll recognize it, Rosemary.*

Secretively he watched as she unwrapped it and broke off a piece, placing it in her mouth. "A ha!" His outburst startled her, and the pie dropped out of her hand, onto her lap. "Please tell me, who did you ask about my dislikes and likes? Was it mother? Cook?"

She frowned, then her eyes widened, and she looked at the pie in her lap and spat the piece out her mouth "You sneaky—" she began.

"I thought you hated pies." He smirked.

"You tricked me!" Angrily, she folded her arms and refused to meet his eyes. "I didn't know it was pie!"

"Oh, give up, would you? You have been caught. I know you have been snooping, trying to find out things about me."

She blushed and looked at him. "Was it that obvious?"

He nodded.

Her shoulders sagged. "I just wanted to get to know you more."

"Don't—It wasn't—"

She lifted her hands, stopping him from going any further. "I know, it wasn't what we agreed."

He didn't like the sad look on her face. She was having doubts about the arrangement, something she had suggested. And he was a fool to think otherwise. After witnessing how loving her parents were, he should have known then that she would want more eventually, more of something he would never be able to give her.

"I think you should go back to the house. The doctor will be here soon, and you shouldn't be present during his visit."

She nodded. Wordlessly she stood, walking to the door before she paused and turned to him. "Cayden?" she said softly. He loved the way she whispered it. "You'll keep me informed about Mystic, won't you?"

"Yes," he assured her. "Of course, I will."

And with a smile, she left.

Inhaling deeply, he looked down to see the foal looking at him. "I know—she's...something." He smiled sadly.

ROSEMARY NERVOUSLY PACED THE drawing room. The doctor had taken his own time, arriving as if a foal's life was naught. It had angered her, as she fretted from worrying about Mystic. She wondered what was being said and done to help the foal. Beth entered the drawing room with a tray of tea and scones. Food helped distract her, and she had eaten an entire pie since retiring to the drawing room. She waved at Beth nonchalantly to place the tray down on the table beside the window, while she continued pacing.

This was torture!

"Beth!"

The girl twirled around, halting from spinning the doorhandle, eyes widening. "Yes, Lady Rosemary Caswell?"

"Let's go to the stables." She grabbed hold of the girl's arm, walking out of the drawing room and towards the stables. "We have to be quiet; my husband and the doctor are in there."

At the entrance of the stables, Rosemary released the girl and stepped forward. Voices travelled towards her, but they were indistinct. Gingerly she moved closer, and then, aware of Beth following, she entered the stall next to Mystic's. It was empty and only filled with stacks of hay. Pressing her ear to the wooden wall, she motioned for Beth to come in the stall.

"Aww, there it is," the doctor exclaimed. "Here's where the animal was in pain."

Mystic was in pain!

"Doctor, did someone hit it?" Cayden's voice was stern and filled with anger.

Heavens, he loves that foal. She wondered if she was injured whether he'd have the same reaction. He'd probably take one look at her and say, *'if it's her will to live, she will. Just give her something to bitter to drink, so she'll die faster.'* Rosemary snorted and quickly covered her laughter, just as Cayden asked what that noise was.

"It's perhaps just one of the horses," the doctor said wearily. "And I believe the mother may have hit it, unintentionally. Happens sometimes, you were right to separate them. Continue feeding...urrrmm..."

"Mystic." Cayden reminded. "My wife named him."

"Quite magical." The doctor chuckled.

"That's what I said!" Rosemary mouth hung open, and she grinned at Beth, who placed her finger on her mouth telling her to be quiet.

"Mystic will be all right. Continue with the feeding until he's well. I'll come by in three days to check his progress."

"Thank you, Doctor." She could hear the relief in Cayden's voice.

The gentlemen were leaving now, and Rosemary, if she knew her husband well, would no doubt peek in the stall. She wasn't convinced he believed the noise was a horse. She grabbed Beth's hands pulling her behind the pile of hay. They crouched on their knees then, just as she suspected, the door opened. Her heart beat excitedly and she bit her bottom lip, concealing a grin. Beth tried to peek and Rosemary smacked her lightly on the head.

"Lord Caswell, are there any other horses you wanted me to take a look at?" the doctor asked.

"No. Thank you for coming. Let me escort you out." The door of the stall closed, and she waited a while before jumping to her feet.

"Do you think we'll get back before him?" She turned to Beth, expectantly.

Beth nodded. "The terrace at the back leads to the drawing room."

"Of course!"

They raced back to the terrace and entered the house. They made it to the drawing room just as the door opened.

"Oh Cayden!" The scone she had stuffed in her mouth, caused her words to be muffled. "What did the doctor say?" She chewed quickly, swallowing the contents. "Is Mystic going to be all right?"

Cayden entered, not taking his eyes off her, he walked towards her. Bending, he started to sniff, and she surged to her feet. "What's the meaning of this? How insolent!"

"I believe you already know what happened to Mystic, since you were there."

She blinked. "I beg your pardon?"

"Oh, save me the theatrics, Rosemary." He sighed, exasperatingly. "I smelt you."

Rosemary chuckled. "You expect me to believe you smell the scent of jasmine and strawberry in a stable filled with horses and their waste?" She cocked her head to the side. "You know what? I'll take that as a compliment."

Cayden rolled his eyes. "I also saw your head!" He pointed at Beth.

Beth looked at her, frightened. The girl was always edgy. Rosemary tried to communicate to her maid, not to say anything, when she did the opposite.

"It wasn't my head—it-I-- was here in the drawing room—we were sewing."

Rosemary placed her hands on her hips and looked to the heavens while Cayden laughter echoed throughout the room. "Fine, we did go to the stables. I see no reason why we should not."

Her forehead creased when Cayden dropped back on the sofa, still bursting with laughter. "She-she—My wife sewing?"

Rosemary groaned. "Come along Beth, I'll have to teach you how to lie."

Chapter Thirteen

"ᴘERFECT!" WITH AN ENORMOUS smile on her face, Rosemary placed the quill on the desk and took her completed work in both hands. Tears sprung to her eyes as she continued to stare at the last word. It had been challenging drafting this book, and she had entered a loveless marriage because of it. Hopefully, one day it would pay off, and she'd have it published in her own name. Rosemary sighed— that would be another challenge. Even as a princess, there were still certain things a lady could and could not do. She placed the book on the desk and started to tap her fingers against the wood. Perhaps she'd ask her husband to submit it in his name, or she could simply wait until her brother was king. Richard would publish her work, and no one would question him. The King of Blackmane was immensely powerful. Even the king of England had seen him as a threat over the years. A treaty had been negotiated that they would not go to war with each other. Her brother becoming king would change things for her. With new determination, she stood and rushed off to her chamber.

She groaned when she saw Hugh leaning his shoulder against her bedchamber door with arms folded.

"What do you want?" she groaned, not hiding her displeasure.

His eyebrows lifted. "A pleasure to see you as well," he said sarcastically, moving to stand upright. "I'm looking for my brother."

"Oh, how surprising," she drawled. "Don't tell me you miss him already."

His nostrils flared. "Don't mock me, Princess. I have something to discuss with him."

"He's not here."

"I am aware of that, that's why I'm asking you where he is." He growled.

"My husband is a grown man, Hugh. He doesn't tell me where and how long he'll be staying." For the past days Rosemary had been occupied with her writing and feeding Mystic occasionally, for her husband had a feeding schedule. She had only seen Hugh once at breakfast. The other days she had taken her meals in the library and her chamber, as she focused on finishing her story. Cayden didn't come to see her once.

Hugh's eyes widened, and his laughter irritated her ears. He wiped an imaginary tear from under his eye. It only showed how heartless he was, and Rosemary wondered how he could ever be related to her husband.

"He hasn't touched you as yet."

She clutched the journal in her hands, as he took a step closer.

"You haven't shared his bed – this is interesting."

"I don't have to listen to this." She took a step forward when he grabbed hold of her arm.

"Why did you marry my brother?"

"I suggest you take your hands off me or you'll have no use of them in the future," she sneered.

It was probably her threat, or the fact that he realized that he had grabbed her that had him releasing her and taking a step back. Rosemary soon realized it was neither when footsteps were heard racing up the steps, and her husband came into view.

"Cayden!" She rushed towards him, and he embraced her. She knew it was because of the presence of his brother, nevertheless she longed for moments like these. Releasing her, he kissed her forehead and smiled down at her. "How are you doing today, my lovely wife?"

"I finished my novel," she exclaimed.

His eyes widened, and he took the journal from her hands. "I must read it."

"No, not as yet." She snatched it back.

Cayden eyebrows creased. "What's wrong?"

"I'm not ready to share it with others."

Cayden nodded then turned to acknowledge his brother. "Hugh, I came as soon as I remembered. I was buying a team of horses, the best breed in the country."

"We have business to discuss. Let's go to the study." Hugh turned and started walking down the hall.

Cayden turned back to her. "You must forgive him. He's not very patient—congratulations on the book."

She watched him go with a sigh. Was he so naïve to his brother's attitude towards him? With a shake of her head, she went inside her chamber.

"WHAT SEEMS TO BE the problem, brother?" Cayden closed the door behind him upon entering the study. He'd almost forgotten about their meeting upon his ride into town to gather more medicines for Mystic and to check on more horses to purchase. The foal was doing much better than before. The doctor was amazing. Cayden was grateful.

Hugh was leaning against the desk, hands folded, regarding him shrewdly. He had learned years ago to ignore Hugh's strange behaviours. The glares that Hugh usually reserved for scaring others didn't affect him.

Cayden smirked. "Did you bring me here to gaze at me like that?"

For a moment, Hugh didn't speak. "I'm starting to doubt myself, whether what I'm about to tell you is a promising idea." At this, Cayden frowned. "But what better time, than when Mother isn't here?" Their mother had left for Bath to visit her sister.

Cayden waited anxiously for his brother to reveal his reason for this hasty meeting.

"I got a letter from Commander Brandell; He needs men. I have enlisted. I want to know if you'd like to join me, but if your duties are here with your wife and those new titles you have inherited, I can completely understand."

Cayden's eyes, which had widened at the mention of Hugh enlisting in the army, suddenly blinked rapidly as his mind began to comprehend the nature of this situation. Hugh knew he was injured, and the topic of enlisting should not be mentioned. An injured man in the army didn't return. And what about his wife? He closed his eyes, resisting the urge to groan aloud. Was he contemplating leaving?

What better way to die than a hero?

But he was a coward.

And what about his wife?

Enlisting would save him the trouble of drinking the poison. On the battlefield he wouldn't be able to hesitate.

But what about his wife?"

Cayden frowned. He shouldn't be thinking about the consequences of leaving her. Not when it had already been planned—marry her, make his mother happy for a while, and then leave this world and his pain of losing his friend. But why was his heart suddenly so reluctant?

"A cripple cannot enter the army," he murmured.

Hugh smiled wryly. Moving towards him, he laid a hand on Cayden's shoulder. "My dear brother, don't think so little of yourself. You walk excellent most of the time. No one would suspect if you continued as you are, but you must understand that I don't wish to force you."

"I know," Cayden whispered.

"We have always enlisted together. Promising that we would watch each other's back."

But Hugh wasn't there to save him when the cannon ball got thrown at him. It was Eric. "I'll think about it."

Hugh lowered his hands, his face almost breaking into a frown. "Don't take forever, we deploy soon."

We, as if he knew his answer already. Hugh give him a gentle squeeze on his shoulder before leaving him standing in the study. Cayden took a seat behind his desk and buried his face in his hands. This wasn't the news he had expected. It should be a blessing, but it was not. He felt reluctant, and he knew why. Marriage was complicating his life; his wife was the sole purpose of it. She had changed, and he was slowly starting to change as well. Rosemary was smart, extremely gorgeous, kind, a siren; Rosemary was dangerous to him. Even more dangerous than the small poison bottle, he hadn't thought of for days.

Chapter Fourteen

ROSEMARY HATED BEING IGNORED. From her chamber window, she watched her husband leave their home. Her husband had not looked upon her or spoken to her for almost two weeks since his meeting with Hugh. What did that man tell him, she wondered, tapping her feet lightly as she watched her husband disappear down the road. Her plans of wooing him were being hindered. How was she supposed to get close to her husband?

"Lady Rosemary?" Beth called, as she entered and closed the door.

Rosemary kept staring out the window. "Beth? How old are you?"

There was a moment before an answer was given. "I'm one and twenty Lady Rosemary."

At this she gasped and turned swiftly around. "You don't look a day over sixteen!"

Beth blushed.

"Come," She held onto the maid's hand, guiding her to sit on the bed. "Can I trust you, Beth?"

"Of course, you can, Lady Rosemary."

"I want to ask you something personal; And since you are older, you should be able to answer it."

The maid nodded.

"My husband, as you may have already known, is avoiding me. How does one keep a husband entertained?"

Beth eyebrows lifted. "I-I suppose at the dinner table?"

Rosemary frowned. "Surely there's more!" She surged to her feet. "I should have known you'd be too coy to tell me." If Penelope, her uncle Fredrick's daughter, was here, she would not hesitate as Beth was doing. Penelope was as blunt as they come and even just a few years younger than her, knew a lot. "My mother told me what happens on the wedding night—" She stopped and tuned back to Beth. "Do you think that's what's missing?"

But Cayden said there wouldn't be anything of that sort.

Beth slowly nodded. "I was told that when a man is denied —" Beth inhaled and exhaled deeply. "They take mistresses."

"Mistresses!" Rosemary started to pace. Would Cayden? Her heart started to thud, she could not remember if in a marriage of convenience, it was accepted or if they had agreed—she shook her head. No! she wouldn't agree to such a thing. Cayden never slept out, except in the stables, and she released a sigh of relief. "Cayden wouldn't," she said softly then paused to stare at Beth. "Where is he going?"

"The stables."

She nodded, content with that answer.

THE EVENING SOON TURNED into night, and though she had pleaded with him to have dinner with her, he refused, claiming he had to feed the horses for the night. They had servants for that! Stablehands, who were rarely in the stables and more likely to be found in the kitchen! Rosemary groaned as she kept tossing and turning in bed. What was she to do? She longed for his attention, his smiling eyes, even his bickering. A noise suddenly caught her attention. She sat upright and waited. The noise wasn't heard again, except for the one outside. Quickly, she rushed to the window and saw her husband walking beside a horse. It was dark, but she recognized his form and mannerisms. Hurriedly she got dressed and put on her favourite beige cloak. She went to the stable and took one of the horses she brought from Blackmane. It wasn't difficult to catch Cayden. He walked until he was further from the estate before mounting his horse.

What was all the secrecy? Did he really have a mistress?

"I'll find out," she mumbled, mounting her horse as well and urging it into a gallop. She thought he was going into town, but he stopped by a small house and entered. Blinking back tears, she stopped. Her head sank at this betrayal. She turned the horse back to the estate.

Rosemary didn't stop crying as she entered the house and headed to her chamber. One by one she peeled the clothing off her body as her sobs echoed in the still chamber. She climbed into bed, but no matter how she pleaded for sleep, it would not come. But her husband did. She heard the heavy footsteps, as they swept past her chamber. Furious, she surged out of bed and entered his chamber through the adjoining door.

"How dare you!"

Cayden sat in the armchair facing the fire. "Dare I what...wife?" he slurred.

She moved to face him. He had a bottle in his hand and as he placed it to his lips, she snatched it. "How dare you go off to spend the night with your mistress and come back here drunk!"

He stared at her before throwing his head back on the chair. "I don't want to talk, go to bed." His voice was hoarse, as if parched and in need of water or the liquor in her hand. She could bet it was the latter.

"Your drunkenness is no excuse. We'll talk about this now while the servants are asleep." She swallowed back a sob. "Why?"

"What?" His eyes lazily peeked open.

"Is she prettier than me? Do I know her?"

"Who?

"The woman you went to meet tonight!" She was getting mighty irritated.

"When?"

"This very nigh—" She stopped when she caught his lips trembling, surmising a smile. "Cayden, I'm serious!"

"You believe I have a mistress? Or would dream of having one when I'm married to you?"

"Are you trying to say if it was some other lady besides me, you would have?" she stated in disgust.

"I didn't---" He leaned forward; his face buried in his hand. "Christ, my head is pounding and not from the liquor."

"That's what happens when you are drunk." She moved to place the bottle on the small table near the window. "I need answers." She returned, standing before him, arms folded.

"I told you I don't have a mistress. Why would I? If word got out, your entire family would have my head!"

"You do have one, but no one knows except me! You are keeping her hidden because of my family."

Cayden groaned.

"How could you do this? I know I forced you into this marriage, but at least show me some respect. Wait until after I retired to the countryside, which I'll be doing very soon, I might add."

He stood, swaying slightly and a startled gasp escaped her lips when he cupped her cheeks in his hands. He leaned in slightly and captured her lips. At first he kissed her slowly as if hesitant to hurt her before demanding more. Just as the other times he had kissed her, Rosemary couldn't think, and she wrapped her arms around him, drawing him nearer.

He moaned, as he started exploring her body with his hand. His palm rested against one of her breasts and she gasped, pushing him away slightly. "Cayden--?"

"Do you want to know what I was thinking about for the past weeks, which got me so drunk?" He pulled her towards him and started to kiss her once again until her head spun. He scooped her up in his arms and miraculously walked towards the bed without dropping her. Rosemary looked at him when he laid her on the bed. His eyes were dark and still drunken, but it wasn't the liquor. His lips touched her collar bone, moved towards her neck before capturing her lips. Her chemise was bunched at her waist, and he ran his hands along her soft skin.

Her breath caught in her throat when he touched her, and she grabbed the sheets when he entered her with his fingers. "Oh!" Her heart felt like it would burst, then when he took one of her breasts and started suckling it, she cried out and he went still.

No! She didn't want him to stop.

His head lifted, and he stared at her before terror marked his face. He leaped off her and took a step back. "Dear heavens, this can't happen. This is –what I'm I doing?" He held his head.

Rosemary sat upright on the bed, hugging her trembling knees. She didn't know what to say and kept her head lowered.

"Did-did I hurt you?"

She shook her head.

He stood there for a minute watching her before his footsteps retreated. She thought he was leaving but when she heard a thud, her head lifted and she raced off the bed to find him laying on the floor with the rest of the liquor around him.

Chapter Fifteen

*C*AYDEN AWOKE TO THE relentless pounding in his head. He groaned and tried to move his hand to rub at his forehead, but something heavy was hindering it from that task. He frowned, turning to see what the devil was wrong with his hand. Then he saw her. Rosemary lay on his hand, long lashes, brushing against her cheek, mouth slightly ajar.

He blinked and turned back to stare at the ceiling, trying to remember what transpired last night. His free hand travelled absentmindedly over his fully clothed body. Nothing of that sort happened last night, thank heavens! But he felt a pang of disappointment. She was his wife and if he wasn't so adamant about taking his own life, he would have loved to hold her in his arms, and give her the marriage she deserved. Turning to gaze at her, he reached out to caress her cheek, brushing wisps of hair away and tucking it behind her ear. He should have let her marry a prince instead.

"I'm truly sorry...." His voice croaked. "But even I cannot be that selfish."

Cautiously he removed his hand from beneath her and climbed out of bed. As he stood the world started to spin. He closed his eyes, waited momentarily before taking a step forward. His feet collided with a bottle, sending it rolling across the room, and he cursed silently.

"Cayden?"

He closed his eyes on a sigh, before turning to gaze at her.

"Are you feeling all right?"

"Yes, quite well," he lied. Her eyebrows creased, and he was certain she knew he was lying. Unable to keep staring at her in his bed, he looked away.

"All right," she said softly. He heard shuffling and then footsteps. "I'll get back to my chamber. Beth will be coming soon." As she swept past him, he closed his eyes, resisting the urge to pull her back into his arms. "Cayden?"

He turned to her, and she stared back. Her mouth opened to say something, but she thought otherwise and shook her head.

"Wait!" he shouted when she turned to open the adjoining door. She swung back around. "What were you about to say? And tell me, why...why did you stay?"

Her eyes widened. "You can't remember?"

He said nothing.

Her shoulders sagged. "I-I had a terrible dream and you told me that I could spend the night." Her smile didn't quite reach her eyes.

He scratched his nape, and his eyes found the bottle on the floor. "I was drunk." He seldomly drank, for he detested headaches and occasional memory loss. It helped for a while, especially when he wanted to forget about Eric, but he always remembered. Then the pain came back as fresh as it was that day, and it was torture.

"Which is probably why you allowed me to stay." She chuckled. "Farewell." She was out of his chamber before he could ask any more questions.

His valet, Aros, entered a few seconds later, catching him staring at the door.

"Good morning, my lord," He stopped short, lips parted in surprise. "What happened to your attire?"

Unconsciously, Cayden smoothed his wrinkled waistcoat.

"That's not what I left—" His valet stopped talking and suspiciously stepped forward and took a deep breath. "You were drinking heavily again."

"I guess I couldn't sleep."

"You usually go to the stables or indulge in the study," his valet said, helping him out of his waistcoat. "Not visit that drunkard's cottage. I should have a word with him for still giving you liquor."

Cayden rubbed his forehead he went to the old gardener's cottage. How desperate had he been to get Rosemary out of his mind? His old gardener, who lived near to the estate, always welcomed Cayden, not because he was once his employer but the prospect of a drinking partner, whenever he appeared. "He's just lonely. You should visit him sometime, noticeably quiet and only moves his mouth to drink."

The valet's nose wrinkled causing Cayden to laugh.

CAYDEN WAS IN THE stables, brushing Mystic's mane, when the sound of giggling drifted towards the him. His wife was back from her travels to town, something she had been doing for the past days with her lady's maid. His mother had accompanied her once, before returning to her sister's estate. He frowned. His wife didn't have many friends except for her cousins whom she spoke fondly of. Perhaps, they should host a ball. The brush stopped stroking Mystic, and he shook his head. It was too early for a ball. Besides, in the eyes of society, they were newlyweds and wouldn't or shouldn't have time to plan those sorts of things yet. The laughter grew until his wife raced into the stables, a vison of pink and white ribbons, her curly hair hidden under a beige bonnet. She stopped immediately upon seeing him and her smile brightened.

"Cayden!" She rushed towards him and for a second, he thought she was going to embrace him and his heart soared, before plummeting to the ground when she went on her knees, wrapping her arms around Mystic, and raining kisses on the foal. He had never been more jealous of a horse.

"Mystic! I miss you so much!"

"Lady Rosemary Caswell!" Beth came into the stables, gasping for breath with a basket in hand. "You are quite fast!" When she saw him, she curtseyed and greeted him as well.

"I am quite aware." She grinned and reached for the basket.

Cayden stood aside and watched as she fed the horse the apples, she brought back from town.

"Did you bring back anything for me?" he said sharply.

Rosemary head snapped up at him, and she climbed to her feet, dusting straw from her gown. "You didn't inform me that you wished for me to."

"Neither did the horse," he retorted.

She smirked. "Why, my lord, you aren't jealous are you?"

"Ha! Me? Jealous of a horse? Don't be absurd." He patted Mystic's mother.

"Am I?" She took an apple from the basket, opened her palm and watched as Mystic's mother took the apple.

Sometimes, he forgot she was a princess. He'd known many women who would shriek at being in the stables and getting dirt on their gowns.

"Besides, I didn't go shopping today. We went for a walk."

"But you took the carriage."

"Indeed, and when we reached Height Creek, we started to walk."

"Height Creek!" His loud shout caused the horses to neigh. Rosemary merely blinked at him. "Do you not know the dangers of that creek? People disappear along that path!" He turned to Beth. "And you! You allowed this?"

Rosemary stepped in front of Beth protectively. The maid looked like she was on the verge of crying. "Beth has nothing to do with this." She folded her arms. "And I am excellent at taking care of myself. The creek was no danger."

"I forbid you from going back there."

"Why? You don't care."

His teeth gritted. He did care, dammit! More than she knew. More than he would like to admit. And he didn't like the feeling of her in danger.

"I'm feeling quite tired and believe I'll retire for the rest of the evening." She walked quickly out of the stables. Beth looked at him nervously before racing to catch up with her.

～┼～

ROSEMARY HAD JUST CLOSED her eyes after lying awake for hours thinking about her husband, when a loud shout sounded from his chamber. She was already across the room, pulling the door open. "Cayden! Cayden!"

He was on the floor, lying flat on his stomach, with his hands protectively over his head. "Cayden, are you all right?" On her knees, she hesitantly reached out to touch him, but he startled her when he immediately sat up and brought her into a bone crushing hug. He buried his head in her neck and didn't move. Rosemary wanted to know if she should as well, before eventually wrapping her arms around his broad shoulders.

"Cayden? Do you wish to talk about it? If you speak about a nightmare, you won't dream of it again, nor will it come true because you won't be alone for when it comes again."

He stiffened in her arms, lifted his head, and just gazed at her. His hands reached out to touch her cheek but fell back to his side.

"I don't need to prove that you are real and safe."

She smiled at his words.

"Because only you, alone, would say something so naïve and think life is full of fairy tales."

At this her smile faded.

He moved away from her and stood. "It's not, Rosemary, and the sooner you learn that, the better it will be. So you will stay out of danger."

"You are talking about my visit to Height's Creek?" She surged to her feet. "The carriage driver was there too, which I must remind you is one of my guards. Nothing would have happened to me. And I know you don't care, so don't pretend to!"

"I don't care?!" He took her by the arms. "You have no idea." He then released her, running his hands through his hair.

"Well, tell me! You hardly spoke to me over the past days or even cared to look at me! This is not how a marriage is supposed to be!"

He shook his head. "I should have known you wouldn't be able to stick to your own plans." He chuckled nastily. "Is this what young, desperate ladies are doing nowadays? Lying just to trap a man into marrying her?"

Rosemary blinked, too stunned to do anything. It was the truth. She had been desperate, and she had been hoping for more, going against her words. Tears started to fall on her cheeks. "You are indeed right, I have not kept my word. I wanted more from this marriage, but I didn't mean to make you feel trapped and miserable. It's all my fault--I cannot stand the thought of someone being unhappy with me, and for that I'm sorry. I won't bother you again, my lord."

She started to walk away when he said, "You are not the one at fault. I, too, entered this marriage—"

"Because I forced you." She closed her eyes, the weight of it suddenly weighing on her chest. "I need to know. Did you seek me out the day after the ball because you found out who I was? Did my royal title prompt your agreement?"

They stared at each other for a while. "Yes, someone had told me who you were, and I pretended not to know. But would it had made a difference?"

She gave him a watery smile. "T-thank you for your honesty."

Chapter Sixteen

OR THE PAST NIGHTS, Rosemary had cried herself to sleep and during the day, she would stare off into nothing, thinking about the repercussions of her actions. Richard always warned her about her haste to make rash decisions. He said she only thought about the present, not the distant future. She was more upset at her stupidity than Cayden's deceit because she deserved it. What lady proposed marriage to a gentleman? Manipulated him into marrying her? So how could she be mad at him when everything he said was the truth?

"Lady Rosemary!" Beth entered the chamber bursting with energy. "We have guests!"

Rosemary buried her face in the pillow, reluctant to play hostess.

"It's Mr. Jude Yale and the Marquess." She pulled the drapes aside, allowing the bright stream of light to enter.

Rosemary groaned and turned on her back.

"Oh, how handsome the Marquess is when he isn't drunk!" she enthusiastically said.

Rosemary turned to her maid, who stared dreamily out the window. Annoyed, she sat upright and threw her pillow at Beth, who shrieked and turned towards her. "Help me get dressed." She'd had enough with ladies acting hopelessly romantic about gentlemen. She was turning into a bitter old lady, and she didn't care.

Beth got her dressed quickly, too quickly, and soon she greeted the gentlemen in the drawing room.

Jude stood, taking her hands, and bringing it to his lips. "Your Highness, how are you faring this morning?"

Despite everything, she smiled at his charm. "Mr. Yale, tis always a pleasure." She turned to the other gentleman. She knew him from her wedding, but unlike Mr. Yale, they had not had a proper conversation. Beth was right, the Marquess was handsome. He smiled at her sincerely or at least tried to for his brown eyes looked like he'd been weeping for days.

"Your Highness." He bowed, and she jumped back with a start when he pulled a single rose from his sleeves.

"Oh, how delightful!" She chuckled.

"A rose for a rose." He grinned.

"Thank you." Rosemary smiled. Inhaling the flower, she wished her husband was as charming as this. "Please have a seat."

They waited until she took hers before filling the chairs. "I trust you are looking for my husband, but I'm afraid he's not at home."

"That would have been a problem, if we had come to call on him."

She looked at Jude in astonishment. "Why, I'm honoured."

"Don't flatter me, Princess—"

"Please call me, Rosemary." She turned to the Marquess. "The both of you."

The gentlemen looked at each other, before shaking their heads. "For our own safety, I don't believe we can," The Marquess, said. "Would Lady Caswell be more suitable?"

"That would be just fine," she replied. "Now tell me gentlemen, what is it you wish to discuss?"

Jude sighed. "Your husband--"

She frowned.

"---I want to know if anyone contacted him regarding his regiment?"

"I-I I'm not sure—" Rosemary stuttered at the thought of Cayden in the army again. "He hasn't mentioned anything of the sort."

"He would not return if he followed them."

"What makes you think he would follow?" she asked.

"Because his disgusting brother would, and we are afraid he'll talk Cayden into it."

Good. Someone else hated Hugh as much as she did. "Cayden's injured; would he not be rejected?"

"His injury is not that severe, and once you are willing, they'll accept you. They need as many men as possible." Jude stated.

"He can decline, can't he?" And she wondered if he would?

"Yes." Jude replied. "No army wants men who aren't committed to the cause, but Cayden, he's –" He hesitated. "Cayden wasn't always like this, vulnerable, distant. It all started when he lost his friend, Eric. It shattered him, and he blamed himself for his death. It's made him who he is now, but not what he was meant to be— Don't give up on him Rosemary."

"I'm afraid it's too late. He didn't want to be in this marriage, but I forced him and now he's miserable," she cried.

The Marquess snorted. "He was miserable long before you came, my dear."

Jude nodded sympathetically. "It is the truth. He laments that he survived when his friend didn't. Eric died, and he held himself responsible. He'd been slowly wasting away until he found you."

"I found him, and I suppose you already knew about my proposal, which he only agreed to because of my family." She looked away from Jude's puzzled expression. "I really thought he didn't know who I was before."

"He didn't," Jude inserted.

"There's no need to defend him, Mr. Yale. He already told me the truth."

"He lied," the Marquess stated.

Rosemary frowned.

"None of us knew who you were at first until the letter you sent him."

"We only knew your name was Rosemary, which we had no trouble teasing him about." The Marquess grinned. "We thought he was jesting, agreeing to marry a lady he knew nothing about."

Rosemary's heart was beating too quickly.

"That's how I knew you were special and would be the one to save him," Jude said with a smirked.

She shook her head and stood to her feet. "This doesn't make any sense. Why would he have lied to me?"

"Isn't it obvious?" Jude lifted his eyebrows.

Her eyes clouded with tears. "To push me away."

"Because?" the Marquess, prompted.

"I was getting too close." She slowly sat back in the armchair. *Could it really be true?*

"See? I told you she was smart," the Marquess mumbled.

Jude smiled. "We were hoping to wait until his return."

"Of course, and please stay for dinner," she offered.

ROSEMARY HAD A LOT to think about as she lay in bed. Cayden hadn't returned and Jude and the Marquess, were getting worried. After dinner they left to seek him out. The look on Jude's face before he departed haunted her. He knew something. She turned on her side again. *Please don't do anything rash, Cayden*, she pleaded. She heard laughter, distant but very vivid. Without thinking, she opened her door and raced down the hall. "Cayden?"

She stopped at the top of the staircase, and saw a man sitting on the steps, his back was to her, and he was chuckling.

"I did it!" He brought something to his head and drank it.

"Did what?"

The man brought his hands slowly down and turned to her. It was Hugh. He staggered to his feet, "Aww, the wife," he stuttered. "I thought you'd be the one to ruin my plans."

"What plan?" She folded her arms, suddenly feeling a chill in the air.

Hugh waved his hand dismissively at her. "No worries, he's already gone."

Cayden! Frightened, Rosemary's heart leaped. "What have you done to my husband?"

"Husband?" He laughed, humourlessly. "Can you even call him that when the marriage is not consummated?" He started to step towards her. "Why don't I do what he was not man enough to do?"

Rosemary was already racing the down the hallway when she heard scuffling behind her. "Lady Caswell!"

Jude!

She turned back and met Jude and the Marquess towering over Hugh.

"Are you all right?"

She nodded at Jude, who looked like he wanted to commit murder. "Which ship is he on?"

"Ship?" she asked startled.

The Marquess handed her a letter. "This was waiting for Jude upon his return home. Cayden's gone to join the regiment."

Rosemary took the letter from him, then she read it slowly under the lantern's light. Her knees weak, she fell to the ground. He'd left her. Without a letter or explanation? Everything around her became a blur. Jude was still screaming at Hugh, who was laughing, and the Marquess remained quiet.

"I'm saving him the trouble of drinking that poison. It's more honourable to die on the battlefield than taking the coward's way," Hugh spat.

Poison? Cayden wanted to kill himself? She looked at Jude. "Is this true? Did I drive him to this?" she cried.

"Yes, it is indeed the truth, and it was ever since Eric died." Jude swallowed. "If anyone was at fault, it was me. For I was the one that saved him, when all he wanted to do was die."

The Marquess clapped Jude across the head. "Stop talking nonsense. You did the right thing." He went and crouched on his knees, fisting Hugh's shirt. "You'll tell us which ship he's on, or I'll cut your fingers off one by one."

"You don't scare me, you drunk. It's too late, the ship already left." Hugh grinned.

The Marquess sighed and extracted a knife from his boots. "You need to start answering questions I asked you, and I haven't had a drink for a week. I'm very annoyed."

"It's the truth, Hugh," Jude agreed.

"Which should I start with?" The Marquess grabbed hold of Hugh's hand, while Jude reached down to hold his other hand that had lifted to hit his friend.

"You wouldn't dare!" Hugh growled.

"The ship name's, Hugh," Jude asked.

"Go to hell!"

"Start with the smallest finger," Jude said.

Rosemary thought they were bluffing, but when the Marquess pressed the knife on Hugh's small finger and started drawing blood, she gasped.

"*The Anchor*! Goddammit!"

"See? That wasn't so hard," Jude said, patting Hugh's cheek, mockingly.

"If I find out you are lying..." the Marquess warned, not finishing that sentence.

Both men stood.

"*The Anchor* is a French ship. Some of the regiments are to meet in France, while others are deployed to Spain," Jude said, helping her to her feet. "The next ship doesn't leave until five days from now. I'll have to—"

"No!" She glared. "I'll go. Cayden owes me an explanation, and my family has many ships."

Jude nodded. "You have to leave immediately. What do you wish to do with him?" He looked at Hugh with disgust. "He did try to attack you."

"I'll have my guards hold him until our return," Rosemary said, turning on her heels, she walked away from the trio and Hugh's loud curses. She needed to get to France.

Chapter Seventeen

$\mathcal{I}$T TOOK A WEEK to reach to France, which increased Rosemary's doubts that she was too late. The chance of Cayden still being in France was but a miracle. And she was praying for one now. She stepped off the ship and waited for the guards to clear the path through the clustered crowd. It was her first time on a ship and though she had found out about her sea sickness, a terrible thing, she admitted, it didn't hinder her excitement. It was what kept her from going insane with worry. Beth was also a great distraction—with her storytelling tales of the sea—even though it was the girl's first time at sea as well. Finally in France, she'd explore the city while looking for Cayden. Additionally, she would get to see her Uncle Thomas. They didn't get to inform him of her visit, and she couldn't wait to see the look on his face. The guards managed to hire a coach for her, and they drove to their chateau in France. All the time Rosemary looked out the window, keeping her eye out for Cayden.

To her dismay, she was not successful in glimpsing Cayden. As they left the city behind, and her only view became trees, she settled back in the carriage and fell asleep. Rosemary was awakened in one of the bedchambers in the chateau by hushed voices, around her. She recognized one to be the commander of the guards. She vaguely remembered being carried inside and was too tired to protest.

"My apologies, Your Grace, but the journey was not planned, and thus a letter was not written."

"Very well—and if I get my hands on this gentleman--"

At the second voice, she opened her eyes and sat upright. "Uncle Thomas!"

He turned and smiled that charming smile at her, and she rushed into his arms. "Uncle Thomas, I have missed you!" She pulled away to stare into eyes familiar blue eyes. "You look different." She touched his side of his cheek, feeling the smooth dark hair that grew there. He had not had a beard upon his departure. A year ago her Aunt Clarissa and husband Thomas, the Duke and Duchess of Somerset had left on a miniature tour, she didn't expect them to make France a part of it and meet him so soon. Until her mother revealed one of her correspondences from Aunt Clarissa.

"It's been a long time, Rosemary. A year if I'm correct, and you haven't changed a bit. Still as beautiful." He kissed her on the forehead. "I miss you and the others back in Blackmane and England, of course, but before we start discussing pleasantries, tell me about this scoundrel of a husband."

"Don't get upset." She stepped out of his arms. "He's been misunderstood." On the journey she'd had a lot of time to reflect on what Cayden must have been going through and could only sympathize with him.

"He abandoned you for the army! I know men must do this at times, but this is different. He's injured. It's suicide!"

Rosemary groaned. "I see, the commander has already informed you."

"I was getting ready to visit Clarissa and the children. They are in the south of France to eagerly awaiting my presence. I was at Court when I was told that you were here. I thought it was a jest until I saw you."

She frowned.

He rushed and embraced her. "I'm thrilled, to see you, Rose. I admit I didn't like the circumstances as to why you came—chasing a man halfway across the world weeks after your marriage."

She closed her eyes and sighed, holding on to him a while longer.

"Did he force you to marry him? Had he compromised you?" Thomas cupped her face, staring deeply in her eyes. "Because I'll kill him before he reaches the battlefield."

Thomas had always been protective, so this didn't startle her as much as his fire in his eyes. Over the years, they had created a bond. He treated her like his daughter, and she was forever grateful.

"No, I was the one that forced him." At his confusion, she ushered him to sit beside her on the sofa and told him everything.

When she was finished Thomas groaned, pinching the bridge of his nose. "Rosemary." He exhaled harshly and looked at her with disappointment.

"I'm not the only one at fault. He could have said no." She shrugged, as deep within her heart she was glad Cayden didn't.

"From what you just told me, he did."

"Could have been more adamant." She sighed then grew exasperated at the look he gave her. "Look, what's important is finding my husband, and I need your assistance."

"Dead or alive?"

She playfully smacked him on the arm.

"All right, I'll help, and I trust that you don't wish for your brother to find out about this?" His eyebrows lifted, questionably. "He's at Court, and a very special guest of the King."

Rosemary bit her bottom lip pensively, She didn't wish to face Richard at the moment. As wonderful as it would be to see him, she wanted to find her husband on her own and perhaps when she did, she'd introduce Cayden to him. Richard would only think it was inappropriate to make the journey—chasing a gentleman across the seas. Besides, he was occupied at Court, and she didn't want to distract him from his duties.

She finally shook her head. "No. I do not wish to informed him as yet."

"Very well, we'll start tomorrow." He kissed her on the cheek then stood."In the meantime, you can get some rest and get acquainted with the Chateau. It's filled with lots of inspiration for perhaps another story when all of this is settled." He winked.

She nodded. She needed to find her husband first, only then would she be able to enjoy the ture beauty of France with him by her side.

The following morning, they set out in search of Cayden, they travelled to village after village, dispersing guards here and there, asking even the beggars on the streets. No one knew of any soldiers' camp. It seemed like it was being kept a secret by the King as a protection. After three days of searching, she came to the realization that she was running out of time and her uncle needed to return to his family. She regretted keeping him for such a long period and there was only one thing left for her to do.

Chapter Eighteen

THE SOLDIER'S CAMP WAS torture, as it brought memories of Eric and their times at camps. Awake, Eric tortured him, and at night when he closed his eyes, his wife tortured him. His heart ached with the way he'd left, without even a letter—and his lies. She would be angry, but she would survive without him, then marry someone that could give her a family and her fairytale ending. The thought of her with another man made his fist clench.

He couldn't wait to be on the battlefield, where he planned to leave all his pain and worries. It had been a week since his journey to France and he still hadn't seen Hugh. Perhaps he was in a different company, and they would meet on the battlefield? Or in a different country. He heard numerous wars were taking place in different countries perhaps he joined one of those regimes? Cayden sighed, remembering that he was an enlisted man and not an officer, a disguise to stay hidden. But why was he thinking of his brother? To see him for one last time?

"You'll be sleeping on the battlefield if you don't get some rest, Caswell," the man beside him whispered. It was pitch black in the small tent that accommodated about twenty men. He didn't know who spoke, for they switched places each night, and he was too occupied to pay attention to faces and match them to voices.

"I can't," he whispered.

"Thinking about whether the wife has another man warming her bed?" This brought a series of chuckles in the darkness and Cayden wanted to beat each of them.

"Is that laughter I'm hearing? Soldiers!" At the commander's loud voice, everyone grew still, and the laughter died instantly. "Get out of there, now! On your feet!"

Everyone slid out of the tent and formed a line. The commander passed each of them before stopping at him. "Cayden Caswell?"

"Yes, sir!"

The commander made a disapproving noise. "You are to report to His Majesty's court tomorrow."

Hushed whispers erupted beside him.

He widened his eyes. "What for? And we are to depart tomorrow sir!"

"He's yours." The commander nodded at a tall man before walking away.

Cayden stared at the man, then repeated his questions, but he refused to answer. Instead, he instructed two other men, who stepped out of the shadows, to escort him to the carriage.

"What's the meaning of this!" he shouted.

Pivoting his head, he saw another shadow next to the man looking at him intensely. Cayden snapped his head back to the front. *My gosh, he had eyes like Rosemary.*

Cayden arrived at a chateau the following day. This wasn't the King of France's residence, but he knew they had multiple estates for various pleasures, especially when they wanted privacy from the Court. He stepped out of the carriage and was escorted to the back entrance. They climbed a flight of stairs. Then, to his astonishment, they left him in a large room to freshen up with a set of clothes laid out on the bed and a steaming tub next to the fireplace. He snickered. The king didn't want to meet a dirty soldier that was ready to die to protect his country? After his bath, he was feeling much better. There was a slight knock on the door before a guard entered to escort him downstairs.

Curious, he followed, not that he had a choice. Two large doors swung open to reveal an elaborate dining hall. The young gentleman that sat at the head of the table didn't look like the King of France.

Cayden frowned and his steps faltered. "Who are you?"

The gentleman's eyes narrowed at him. His gaze was intense, and his green eyes shone with fury. It was then he remembered those eyes.

"You were there when I was captured—taken against my will." How did they get here so quickly before him?

The gentleman smirked. "You flatter me, Lord Caswell, for if you were indeed my prisoner, you wouldn't have been able to walk or speak clearly. Please have a seat."

He hesitated, looking at the food then at the mysterious gentleman.

"If I wanted you dead, you would have already been," the gentleman replied.

And Cayden took a seat with a sigh.

"I know the camps don't have much food, and you might be hungry, so I thought we'd get more acquainted over some excellent French cuisine."

He was right about the food. Cayden was hungry and see no reason why he should decline the delicacies before him. He started to eat slowly before stopping. "I can't finish until you tell me why I am here. And why you lied."

"And what exactly did I lie about?"

"I was told the King wanted to see me?"

"Indeed," the gentleman mumbled. "But he's occupied and sent me instead. He has a secret mission for you, but first I need some questions answered."

Cayden nodded with curiosity.

"Tell me about your family. Would they miss you if you disappeared? Are you prepared to lose all contact with them? The assignments would require it."

"I know what's it like to work for the crown," Cayden mumbled. But would he be able to work knowing his wife was back in England and perhaps looking for the next man to marry? Hear rumours of how many children they had? Hopefully he would have died before that. "My mother would be devastated and my brother won't care."

"Your wife?"

At this, Cayden's head lifted.

"I heard rumours that you recently married. What happened to her?"

"I left her." He turned back to gaze into his wine.

"Why?"

"I knew I couldn't give her what she wanted."

"And what is that?"

"Love. Children."

"Why?"

Cayden took large gulp of his wine.

"I need to know everything in order for us to trust you," the gentleman continued.

Cayden's shoulders sagged and he did tell the strange gentleman everything, from his stories about Eric to the day he died. Then he explained about his marriage and why he agreed to wed. The man scowled so hard that Cayden thought he would snap his head any instant.

"You married, with the intention of leaving m—your wife a widow? Just to amuse yourself until it's time!"

"You see why I left? Why I couldn't possibly return. I'm ashamed of myself. It wasn't supposed to go this way dammit!" He banged his hand on the table. "She promised she'd stay away and write her book. We had rules, but somehow they didn't stop my heart from wanting her!"

The gentleman eyebrows lifted at that statement.

Cayden stared at him in shock. "Forgive me, I didn't mean to –"

"To say it out loud?"

Cayden looked away. "I don't know why I said it, it just happened."

"Just like you didn't know that you love your wife."

Cayden frowned. "I didn't say that."

"But you feel it. That's why you ran all the way to France, because you thought that to be happy would betray your friendship with Eric. He lived when you didn't."

"It should have been me," Cayden spat, blinking back tears. "It should have been me," he repeated.

"But it wasn't. You are here for a reason." The gentleman smiled. "You married for a reason; you came to France for a reason. And all those actions are because of your heart. While the others are based off your thinking."

"I don't understand," Cayden said in utter bewilderment.

"You followed your heart when you married—you didn't think. If you had, you wouldn't have married because Eric was in your thoughts. It was because of your heart that you came to France. If you were thinking, you would have known that changing the location of your death doesn't change the outcome. You cannot outrun your heart, so stop. And Eric seemed like a reasonable gentleman and would love to see you happy. Don't ruin what he died protecting."

Cayden stared at the man in astonishment. "Who are you?"

"He's my brother."

Cayden surged out of his chair and turned to stare at his wife. "Rosemary? You—" She was here in France! He turned back to the man, who shrugged at him before standing. Now he was aware of the similarities, seeing them in the same room.

He was Richard, her twin brother, soon to be King of Blackmane.

"I would say it's a pleasure to meet you, but I'll leave that for another day." Richard moved towards Rosemary. "I'll take my leave now and see you in two days." He kissed her cheek before departing.

❧ ✦ ❧

AS THE DOOR CLOSED behind Richard, Rosemary approached her husband, and before she could change her mind, slapped him. "How dare you leave like that! As if we were nothing! I know it was a sham marriage, but I have regarded you as my friend!"

"How could I have faced you? You were the person I was running from. One look at you and I would have stayed. You had made me want to live again when I shouldn't. I am so sorry for causing you much distress. I don't know if I can give you what you wanted."

"It's all right." She pressed her palm on the cheek she had slapped. "I heard everything, you told my brother, and I'm not forcing you to say or do anything. I'll never do that again. What I want is for you to come to me on your own timing. We won't rush anything. Once you are beside me, I'll be content."

Cayden eyes misted, and he brought her to his chest, holding her dearly. "I'm so sorry. I need—I need to get some rest."

She pulled away slightly and nodded, pleased that he was with her. She knew contacting Richard would yield results. She watched him go. If he stayed and didn't return to the regiment, she'd be all right. She must be...

Chapter Nineteen

ROSEMARY SAT STARING AT the brush, Beth had used on her hair. She had Cayden back in her life, but nothing had changed. She knew he could love her; she just needed to be patient. She stood. Leaving the brush on the vanity table, she grabbed the journal off the nightstand and sat on the bed, staring at it. She needed to do something to distract herself.

"I still wish to read your novel."

"Cayden!" Rosemary shrieked. "What are you doing here?"

He closed the door behind him. "This is my wife's chamber; I have every right to be here."

"I suppose you are right." She stood quickly. "I do not have my novel here, I left it at Blackmane. This," she lifted the journal showing it to him, "is something I bought here in France."

"You must have been very desperate to leave your precious novel behind."

"Well, I had to arrive before you departed to the battlefield," she muttered.

"I have a feeling you would have travelled to that said battlefield." He quirked an eyebrow in the air, as he took slow steps towards her.

"Richard would not have let me."

"Could he really have prevented you?"

She blushed and shook her head. "I wanted to visit the camp, but he didn't let me. I was going to escape, only to find out that guards were at my bedchamber door."

"This person must be very fortunate to have you."

"He should think so."

At this, he chuckled and reached out to touch her cheek. Her heart was pounding, and her entire body grew heated under his gaze.

"He knows." His fingers left her cheek, travelling down in a slow tantalizing way to rest against her heart. Rosemary could not breathe. She stood still, eyes widening at him, as his gaze drifted to where his hand lay. He pulled at the strings of her chemise and then looked up at her.

"You must breathe, if you are to live through this." He grinned.

"I—I thought you needed rest?" she said.

He leaned to whisper in her ear. "Yes. And I did, so I can give you my full attention tonight." He kissed her cheek. "That's if you'll accept me?" And as he searched for the answers in her eyes, Rosemary answered, by standing on her toes and capturing his lips.

Cayden kissed her with equal hunger. Quickly, he scooped her up in his arms and lowered them both on the bed.

***

"Cayden!" Rosemary awakened in a state of panic, when she found Cayden missing from her chamber. The sun hadn't risen yet. He was gone, she knew it. Felt it. Further confirmation was a visit to his bedchamber. She raced down the carved stone steps, stumbling as she did. The guards saw her and quickly opened the door. The pre-dawn chill greeted her as she raced across the lawn. The grass prickling at her skin, she finally fell to her knees staring at the wide expanse of land, her chest heaving in exhaustion.

"Lady Caswell!"

Beth stopped behind her.

"He's gone, Beth," Rosemary cried. "He—went back to the army." She lowered her head and sobbed, hands covering her face. She stayed there for a while, hoping, waiting, until Beth stepped forward and helped her to stand.

"Let's get you back to your chamber."

Where she'd stay alone. Sobbing with her loss and grief. "No." She shook her head. "I'm going for a walk."

Beth started to walk beside her when she stopped her. "No Beth, I need to be alone."

The maid nodded.

And slowly Rosemary made her way through several gardens, past a willow tree, and finally stopping at a field of wildflowers, where she sat, hugging her knees together. What must she do now? She'd be able to stay here with Richard for a while; A year, that's how much time Richard had left in France before his return to Blackmane. Her bottom lip wobbled, as she pictured the disappointed look on her parents' faces. It would be even more heart-breaking than when she had returned, pleading with them to let her chase after her husband. She rested her forehead on her knees and started to sob. After the night they shared, she hadn't expected this to happen. She thought they were getting closer. He was finally willing to spend his life with her.

"France is a beautiful place is it not?"

Rosemary's head jerked up and with a gasp, she surged to her feet, turning to gaze into Cayden's eyes.

Cayden frowned. "Why are you crying?"

Wordlessly, she ran into his arms, sobbing with uncontrollably joy. He embraced her immediately, smoothing her long dark hair.

"I-I thought you left. I thought you left me."

His hand stilled and he pulled her away slightly to look down at her. "I'm not going anywhere, my love," he said, kissing her softly on the forehead. "I don't know what my future holds, but I want to be a part of yours."

"Yes." She nodded eagerly.

"I went for a walk as I usually do every morning. Sorry if I scared you." He caressed her cheek. "I want to court you, Rosemary."

"I think it's a little too late for that." She chuckled.

"I didn't get the opportunity to and what better place to show you how much I love you than France?"

Her eyes widened and her heart fluttered with love.

"I love you, Princess Rosemary of Blackmane." He pressed his forehead to hers and repeated the first three words just as the sun rose on the horizon.

Epilogue

QUILL TO PAPER, ROSEMARY sat in one of the lavish gardens at Blackmane castle, starting another story. Returning to England, they had decided to spend some time at Blackmane Castle. The tranquility of it all was exactly what she and Cayden needed. Lifting her head, she smiled, watching her husband picking roses with Ruby, her sister. Since their arrival Ruby had stuck to Cayden, journeying everywhere with him. She smiled faintly, wondering if she should go and save him. Ruby could be such a nuisance at times.

"He's very patient." Rosemary looked up to see her mother's smiling gaze on Ruby and Cayden with a basket in hand. She had gone to pick apples earlier. "You must inform him that there's no harm in saying no."

Rosemary groaned and turned to look at them once again. "I have. I guess it's hard to say when he's met face to face with Ruby. Besides, she doesn't know what the word no means."

Her mother laughed. "You are certainly correct, and you don't either. But it's a fortunate that your unladylike characteristics have given you such a loving husband."

This caught her attention. Startled, she looked up at her mother. "Mother! How long have you known?"

Her mother looked down at her with a warm smile. "It wasn't difficult to notice. I was indeed worried but now, I see how so much in love the both of you are, I am delighted."

"Mama!" Ruby was skipping towards them with Cayden following. When she reached their mother, she stuck her index finger out. It had a small prick. "Look, and not crying!"

Her mother told her how brave she was and took her back to the castle.

"Another story?" Cayden came and sat beside her on the ground.

"Yes. A lady in love has endless ideas worth writing." She grinned.

"Oh, well you are very fortunate to have me for inspiration. Convenient, wouldn't you say?" And with a warm smile, he pulled her in his arms for a kiss.

Acknowledgments

Many thanks and love to:

My Editor and Formatter, Tamara Eaton for her keen eyes, for catching those grammar errors and making this book reader friendly.

My family and friends for the support they have shown.

The cover designer Broken Candle Book Designs thank you for another beautiful cover!

Also, to all my readers, thank you so much for reading *Convenient Beauty*.

Preview:

Hidden Beauty

If you enjoyed *Convenient Beauty*, read on for a preview of Book One of the Beauty Regency Romance Series, *Hidden Beauty*, Sapphire and Damien's story.

London, 1816

SAPPHIRE HERSBERRY FLINCHED and withdrew her hand from the ruby rose she was trying to pluck. She sat back on her knees. Her lips pressed together at seeing the tiny spot of blood on her index finger growing larger by the second. It was not the first time she had been bitten by the thorns of the roses. But each time felt like the first. The pain and sight of blood always caused nausea to arise in the pit of her stomach.

"Another prickle?" Sapphire's nose wrinkled as she nodded at her sister, Mary, who was walking toward her at a leisure pace on the grey flat patches of stones that burst through the middle of the garden. Dry leaves, twigs, and petals that had been swept by the wind, covered the surface like a blanket.

Mary sat beside Sapphire, placing her basket on the ground, then her hand reached out to grab Sapphire's. "I swear, you have more prickles than ladies who handle a needle at the fireplace." Sapphire's eyes lifted to her sister's kind blue orbs. It always startled her, the resemblance between them and their mother's. So similar, but yet each held such different emotions when looking at her.

Sapphire snorted. "I would never spend so many hours indoors." Withdrawing her hand, she wiped the injured finger on her skirt, not caring for the stain it might leave. The gown was outdated and worn, with its brown colouring, No one would notice it anyway. "It would suffocate me to death."

"I know it would," Mary agreed, reaching to pluck the rose that had bitten her sister, the only one that was alive on the bush. "It's very difficult to get you to spend time indoors as it is. I admire that about you, Saf." She twisted the stem of the rose between her thumb and forefinger. "You even saved a life with the flowers and herbs you collect." Mary lifted her gaze and what Sapphire saw in the depths of those blue orbs warmed her heart.

"I couldn't have done it without your help. Besides, what sort of sister would I be if I didn't try to save your future husband?" Mary's cheeks heated with a pink glow that made Sapphire chuckle. Sapphire had seen Charles when he accompanied his father to work on the Hersberry's strawberry field. She knew Mary was attracted to him by the way she volunteered to accompany them in her best dress. Who goes to work in a dress fit for a Ball? Her teasing that day had earned her an unladylike stuck out tongue from Mary.

Charles had taken ill a few days after, and from what Mary had told Sapphire, he preferred to be indoors reading. He had only come to see Mary. Sapphire had sent some herbs for him to make tea, and she had a feeling Mary bringing them cheered him to full recovery.

"Sapphire, don't tease me." Sapphire smiled, peeking inside the basket Mary fiddled in. "I brought these." Mary picked up a bunch of herbs and placed them on Sapphire's lap.

Sapphire widened her eyes. "Oh, these are wonderful!" she exclaimed, inspecting them one at a time. She had some sage, rosemary and clover already, but would not reveal that to her sister, who was just trying to help and keep her company in the garden.

"Put them away before Mama sees them; you know she doesn't approve, and I don't think I can stand her chattering about witches and what's inappropriate," Mary grunted.

Sapphire sighed wistfully. That wasn't the only thing her mother hated about her. Everything she did irritated her mother. She longed for a loving relationship with her, one that her mother displayed toward Mary and Jane. "I don't know why she disapproves of my dreams and passion, Mary. Doctors use and study herbs all the time. Why is it so different when I collect them?"

Lifting the different flowers in her basket, she placed the herbs at the bottom.

"Because you are a beautiful young lady and Mama hates that."

Sapphire's head snapped around to gape at Mary.

"Oh, don't look at me like that. You actually think she dislikes you because you collect herbs and flowers?"

"No, but I didn't think it's because of my features! How vain!" Sapphire exclaimed.

Mary rolled her eyes and stood, taking the basket with her. She tucked it under her arm. "Do you remember when she cut your hair when you were six years old?"

"Yes," Sapphire, intrigued to know more of what Mary had to say, scrambled to her feet with her own basket and ran to catch up with her sister. "What's that got to do with anything?" Sapphire asked, pressing for a firm answer.

"Sapphire Hersberry, I swear you can be as dumb as a twig sometimes!" Mary's dark blue gown swayed around her feet as she turned abruptly to glare at Sapphire. "She did it because she was jealous. Why? I don't know, but it's no secret that she favours Jane and perhaps thought you'd take her suitors away."

"I'm not interested in suitors. My desires are only to study my herbs and perhaps create a book about them one day that would benefit others."

"And you will," Tucking the basket under her arm, Mary reached out to touch Sapphire's cheek. "I'll even help you draw some of the herbs."

The sound of a carriage caused both ladies to look at the garden's entrance. "Looks like Mama and Jane are back from Ryedale village. Come quickly." Mary grabbed her sister's hand, pulling her out of the garden.

Sapphire took a deep breath at the cold stare she received from her mother, who stood hands on hips, blocking the doorway. Her dark blue eyes finally moved to settle on Mary as they stopped in front of her. "You'll follow this one to your grave, Mary. In this dreadful sun, you are without a bonnet!"

"Mother, we didn't—"

"I don't want to hear your excuse. Now get upstairs and tidy yourself!"

Sad, Sapphire watched as Mary disappeared inside the house. "We didn't stay outside as long as you think, Mother, just collected a few flowers for decoration." She reached inside the basket and took out a bunch of white roses. "These are your favourite."

"Get those things out my face!" With much impatience, Lady Hersberry snatched the roses out of Sapphire's hand.

Her breath left her lungs with a hiss as tiny stabs of knives felt like they were assaulting her injured finger.

The roses went flying behind her, with another startled gasp, Sapphire pivoted her head to gape at the freshly picked roses that decorated the green grass.

Lady Hersberry grabbed hold of Sapphire's arm, dragging her inside towards the dining room. "Now listen to me, you disturbance." Lady Hersberry swung on her heels to face Sapphire, her fashionable green silk gown swinging around her body. "Keep away from my little girl. You are poisoning her mind with all these herbs and fairy tale antics. Look at you." Her eyes flickered to Sapphire's hair then her face. "You have brought so much colour to your face that it's hideous, and you're dragging Mary along with your rebellious ways!"

"I'm sorry, Mother but I hate wearing bonnets." Sapphire loved to feel the wind through her hair, making the tresses caress her cheeks.

"For the next three days you will be confined to your chamber, and when you go outside after that time period, wear a bonnet! Don't make me see you without one. Get those herbs you are hiding out of my house! Don't let me find them anywhere in this house." With one last menacing glance, Lady Hersberry swept past Sapphire.

With tears in her eyes and slumped shoulders, Sapphire went back out to the garden to dispose of her herbs. On her way, she picked up the roses her mother discarded. Why does she hate me so much? She refused to believe what Mary told her. There had to be something more to this never-ending hatred.

About the Author

Asata Benjamin lives with her family on the beautiful Island of St. Vincent and the Grenadines, In the Caribbean region and enjoys writing and reading different Romance genres, although her passion dwells on Historical Fictional Romances and Mysteries. *Convenient Beauty* is her third officially publish Historical fictional Romance novella and certainly would not be the last! She is currently working on the other books in this series among other books of different genres.

When she isn't writing, which is very rare, she keeps occupied by reading, thinking of new ideas and spending time with family and friends.

She loves reading, writing, taking pictures of anything that's fascinates her-especially nature. She's also a dedicated pizza eater!

Asata loves hearing from readers. You may contact her and learn more about her works by visiting www.Kademete.com